FAQ About
Translation
Skills-Basic

中英互譯
筆譯技巧

基礎

連緯晏 Wendy Lien、Matthew Gunton ◎ 著

3步驟 超快速入門中英互譯！

迅速解決翻譯時會碰上的多種疑難

培養基礎中英互譯能力＋累積翻譯實力！

❶ 首先由常見Q&A 找出想解決的問題！

❷ 吸收【技巧提點】、實際做【翻譯小小演練】、檢視【解析】，突破困境！

❸ 深入一點看【還能怎麼翻】，強化對翻譯技巧的印象！

重點特色還有……

▌規劃Part 1 中翻英、Part 2 英翻中雙篇，少一些翻譯理論，
只給精簡、扼要的技巧提點，增加易學度！

▌沒有繁重的技巧解說，先從簡易的實戰練習著手，
減輕入門學習者的負擔，加強學習效果！

▌體會翻譯時，轉換中英文語言的無窮樂趣！

PREFACE
作者序

　　我對翻譯熱愛的程度，不可言喻。已從事中英翻譯多年的我，至今仍抱持多閱讀、多聽、多請教、再進步的學習態度，在翻譯的路上努力著。

　　很開心於 2015 年 7 月出版第一本分享翻譯技巧的著作:《Open Your 中英互譯邏輯腦》，並且於一年後，再次與倍斯特出版社合作本書。

　　這次要與讀者分享的基礎翻譯技巧，以短篇文章切入要點，沒有過度修飾的詞藻，而是用精確流暢的譯文，提供學習英文與翻譯入門者，最簡要明確的概念。從基本的辨別英文時態、中英文標點符號運用、中英文語序架構，以及如何將文意的意境與情緒，導入譯文的呈現方式。

　　再此要特別感謝全力協助我完成本書，在台灣有豐富英語教學資歷的先生（Matthew Gunton），以及寫作期間的各方靈感來源:我的兩個兒子 Ashley 艾訒 & Blake 雅各、families in England、親友、學生。

　　希望你能以無預設立場的欣賞角度來消化書中的每篇文章，掌握基本技巧，堅守翻譯的不可違教條－忠於原文，便能達到厚植翻譯能力、精進寫作實力的效果。

作者 連緯晏 Wendy Lien

EDITOR'S WORDS

編者序

　　翻譯的學問永遠探究不完；語言轉換的妙趣無窮無盡。繼《Open Your 中英互譯邏輯腦》以較為進階的教學角度出版後，編輯部便不斷思考如何提供讀者更好的翻譯學習方式。為了能讓翻譯的基礎入門者也能體會翻譯的樂趣，新書企劃因而誕生。

　　不同於上一本教讀者由 8 大主題短文，先透過【英譯中】著手，再推進至【中譯英】的練習與解析、討論，磨練翻譯技巧，本書以「這句中文怎麼翻成英文？」的疑問為出發點，將【中譯英】大篇章放在前頭，並整理出常見的翻譯問題，致力於幫助讀者深耕基礎的翻譯能力，如掌握英文文法、句型和時態的用法；為了翻得正確、不偏離原意，精確使用英文文法、句型與時態，是累積翻譯實力的第一步！

　　在第二大篇章【英譯中】裡，作者率先討論中英文語序的問題，再一步步切入文化背景、補譯、逐字翻譯等翻譯技巧，於一問一答、翻譯練習與解析中，幫助讀者建立正確的翻譯概念。

　　不論是【中譯英】，或是【英譯中】，都是翻譯學習者會碰上的，也才會有雙篇的規劃，同步、獨立學習都很適合。感謝作者撰寫本書時去蕪存菁，只提供最簡要、明白的概念，一切都是為了提高入門學習者的學習效率，更是對於翻譯的信心。

編輯部 敬上

CONTENTS
目次

PART I 中翻英技巧

Chapter 1 英文翻譯句型文法要注意！-1

Chapter 2 英文翻譯句型文法要注意！-2

Chapter 3 容易混淆的英文時態

Chapter 4 中英文語法相通、相異處

Chapter 5 簡化英文句的秘訣、強調英文語氣

PART II 英翻中技巧

FOREWORD

前言

　　本書旨在提供自修與訓練翻譯技巧，以中英雙向互譯要點，厚植寫作與翻譯能力的實力。

　　全書共分成兩個部分：第一部分中翻英；第二部分英翻中，各２４篇文章，共計４８篇。

　　訓練譯文寫作方式的文章內容，以融合日常時事，並配合以下重點做規劃：英文文法結構（現在式、過去式、現在完成式、過去進行式、比較級、假設語氣……等）、句子與上下文的關係、中英文語序、使用適當的連接詞（依語意，適時加入符合前後文語意的連接詞，如「又」、「但」、「而且」……等）、英文片語、英文慣用語、中文成語。

　　每篇文章皆有提供學習者練習翻譯寫作的句子，並在解析與技巧提點中，統整容易誤譯的語詞或英文慣用語、片語。

　　解析精闢概要，有助加強並建構重要觀念。以中英文對照的學習方式，避免理解文意的閱讀盲點。

作者 連緯晏 Wendy Lien

INSTRODUCTIONS

學習特色與使用說明

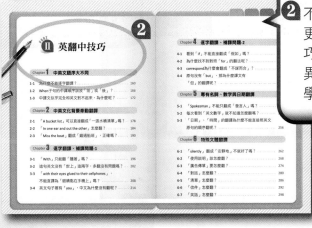

❶ 以必掌握的翻譯基礎要訣，做為大單元的分類，並整理出常見的翻譯問題，立即找到翻譯盲點，對症下藥！

❷ 不僅要學「中翻英」，更要學「英翻中」技巧，中英文的相似、相異處，互有關連，一起學，加深印象！

❸ 關於翻譯的疑難【Q】和解決問題的關鍵技巧【A】，一目瞭然！用關鍵例句小試身手！

❹ 實際小練習前，先看看技巧提點，做暖身！

❺ 試著翻畫底線的部分，也想想本單元重點，並朝重點來努力！

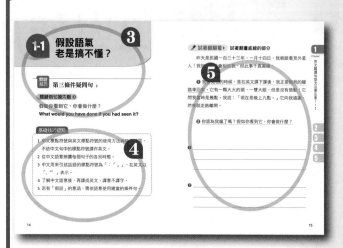

1-1 假設語氣 老是搞不懂？ ❸

關鍵技巧 第三條件疑問句

關鍵例句搶先看 ❷
假如你看到它，你會做什麼？
What would you have done if you had seen it?

基礎技巧提點：
1 中文標點符號與英文標點符號的使用方法與中文不同，不依中文中的標點符號譯作英文。
2 從中文語意辨讀每個句子的各別時態。
3 中文用來引述話語的標點符號為「：」，在英文以「,""」表示。
4 了解中文語意後，再譯成英文，譯意不譯字。
5 若有「假設」的意涵，需依語意使用適當的條件句。

試著翻翻看 試著翻畫底線的部分
昨天是民國一百三十三年、一月十四日，我親眼看見外星人！我發誓我會相信我，但此事千真萬確。

❶ 我看見它的時候，是在英文譯下課後，我正要騎我的腳踏車回家。它有一顆大大的頭，一雙大眼，但是沒有眼睛。它問我當時是幾點。我說：「現在是晚上九點。」它向我道謝，然後就走路離開。

❷ 你認為我瘋了嗎？假如你看到它，你會做什麼？

你翻對了嗎？
❶ 我看見它的時候，是在英文譯下課後，我正要騎我的腳踏車回家。
I was riding my bike home after English class when I saw it.

❷ 你認為我瘋了嗎？假如你看到它，你會做什麼？
Do you think I'm crazy? What would you have done if you had seen it?

❻ ❻

為什麼這樣翻 1

　　配合英文語法，這句話可以拆解成：事情的時間＋此事同時發生的事→「我正要騎我的腳踏車回家是在英文譯下課後」＋「我看見它」。

　　分析上句中文語意後，其采構為：過去進行式＋過去式。以英文語法譯作：
(1) 主要子句（主詞＋過去式 be 動詞（was）＋動名詞（riding）＋地方副詞（home）＋時間片語（after English class）
(2) ＋從屬連接詞（when）＋從屬子句（I saw it）。

為什麼這樣翻 2

　　「你認為我瘋了嗎？」為現在式，現在式表示每天或常態的事。

　　「假如你看到它，你會做什麼？」為第三條件句疑問句，用假設或改變過去來可能完成的事。此句文法公式為：
(1) 代名詞受詞（What）＋would＋主詞（you）
(2) ＋現在完成式（have done）＋if＋過去完成式子句（you had seen it?）。

❻ 答案清晰，並有解析，了解為什麼這麼翻！

❼ 從書側索引也能迅速找出要看的單元！ ❼

16　17

❽ 🖊 也可以這麼翻

❶ 我看見它的時候，是在英文課下課後，我正要騎我的腳踏車回家。

When I saw it, I was riding my bike home after English class.

| 為什麼還能這樣翻 1

也可以英文語法譯作：從屬子句（When I saw it）＋英文逗號（,）＋主要子句（I was riding my bike home after English class）。結構為——從屬連接詞（when）＋過去式的從屬子句（主詞＋過去式動詞＋受詞）＋英文逗號（,）＋過去進行式的主要子句（主詞＋過去式 be 動詞（was）＋動名詞＋地方副詞＋時間片語）。

❷ 你認為我瘋了嗎？假如你看到它，你會做什麼？

Do you think I'm crazy? If you had seen it, what would you have done?

❽ 從「還能怎麼翻」，了解其他可能的正確翻法，一邊腦力激盪，同時體會中英文轉換的無窮樂趣！

| 為什麼還能這樣翻 2

第一句為現在式動詞疑問句。第二句則為第三條件句疑問句。If＋過去完成式子句＋英文逗號（,）＋代名詞受詞（what）＋would＋主詞＋現在完成式。

❾ 看全文的翻譯，學習更為完整！

全文翻譯

❾ Yesterday was the 14th of January, 2044. I saw an alien with my own eyes! I know that you won't believe me, but it's true.

I was riding my bike home after English class when I saw it. It had a big head, big eyes but no hair! It asked me what time it was. I said, "It's nine o'clock at night." It thanked me and walked away.

Do you think I'm crazy? What would you have done if you had seen it?

Part I

中翻英
技巧

1-1 假設語氣老是搞不懂？

關鍵技巧 **學會使用第三類條件句疑問句** ▶

關鍵例句搶先看 ▶

假如你看到它，你會做什麼？

What would you have done if you had seen it?

基礎技巧提點

1 中文標點符號與英文標點符號的使用方法與時機不同，不依中文句中的標點符號譯作英文。

2 從中文語意辨讀每個句子的各別時態。

3 中文用來引述話語的標點符號為「：「」」，在英文以「, ""」表示。

4 了解中文語意後，再譯成英文，譯意不譯字。

5 若有「假設」的意涵，需依語意使用適當的條件句。

✏️ **試著翻翻看▸** 試著翻畫底線的部分

　　昨天是民國一百三十三年，一月十四日，我親眼看見外星人！我知道你不會相信我，但此事千真萬確。

　　❶ 我看見它的時候，是在英文課下課後，我正要騎我的腳踏車回家。它有一顆大大的頭，一雙大眼，但是沒有頭髮！它問我當時是幾點。我說：「現在是晚上九點。」它向我道謝，然後就走路離開。

　　❷ 你認為我瘋了嗎？假如你看到它，你會做什麼？

❶ _____

_____

_____

❷ _____

_____

_____

❶ 我看見它的時候，是在英文課下課後，我正要騎我的腳踏車回家。

I was riding my bike home after English class when I saw it.

| 為什麼這樣翻 1 ⋯⋯⋯⋯⋯⋯⋯⋯⋯⋯⋯⋯⋯⋯⋯⋯⋯⋯⋯⋯

　　配合**英文語法，這句話可以拆解成：事情的時間＋與此事同時發生的事**→「我正要騎我的腳踏車回家是在英文課下課後」＋「我看見它」。

　　分析**上句中文語意**後，其架構為：**過去進行式＋過去式**。以英文語法譯作：

(1) 主要子句（主詞＋過去式 be 動詞（was）＋動名詞（riding）＋地方副詞（home）＋時間片語（after English class）

(2) ＋從屬連接詞（when）＋從屬子句（I saw it）。

❷ 你認為我瘋了嗎？假如你看到它，你會做什麼？

Do you think I'm crazy? What would you have done if you had seen it?

| 為什麼這樣翻 2 ⋯⋯⋯⋯⋯⋯⋯⋯⋯⋯⋯⋯⋯⋯⋯⋯⋯⋯⋯⋯⋯⋯⋯⋯⋯

「你認為我瘋了嗎？」為現在式，現在式表示每天或常態的事。

「假如你看到它，你會做什麼？」為第三類條件句疑問句，在這裡疑問句「你會做什麼」，在翻成英文時，要放在前面；由於這個問題是在假設過去如果發生了這件事，你會怎麼做，即表示過去並沒有發生過這樣的事，而且現在也無法扭轉過去已發生的事情。此疑問句的結構公式為：

(1) 代名詞受詞（What）＋would＋主詞（you）

(2) ＋現在完成式（have done）＋if＋過去完成式子句（you had seen it?）。

❶ 我看見它的時候，是在英文課下課後，我正要騎我的腳踏車回家。

When I saw it, I was riding my bike home after English class.

| 為什麼還能這樣翻 1 ....

也可以英文語法譯作：從屬子句（When I saw it）＋英文逗號（,）＋主要子句（I was riding my bike home after English class）。結構為——從屬連接詞（when）＋過去式的從屬子句（主詞＋過去式動詞＋受詞）＋英文逗號（,）＋過去進行式的主要子句（主詞＋過去式 be 動詞（was）＋動名詞＋地方副詞＋時間片語）。

❷ 你認為我瘋了嗎？假如你看到它，你會做什麼？

Do you think I'm crazy? If you had seen it, what would you have done?

18

| 為什麼還能這樣翻 2 ···

　　第一句為現在式動詞疑問句。第二句則為第三類條件句疑問句：If＋過去完成式子句＋英文逗號（,）＋代名詞受詞（what）＋would＋主詞＋現在完成式。

　　Yesterday was the 14th of January, 2044. I saw an alien with my own eyes! I know that you won't believe me, but it's true.

　　I was riding my bike home after English class when I saw it. It had a big head, big eyes but no hair! It asked me what time it was. I said, "It's nine o'clock at night." It thanked me and walked away.

　　Do you think I'm crazy? What would you have done if you had seen it?

假設語氣
還是搞不懂？

**搞懂「與現在事實相反的假設」和「與
過去事實相反的假設」！** ▶

關鍵例句搶先看 ◐

不過要是你今天早上問我想不想當一隻鳥，也許我的
答案會有所不同。

**But if you had asked me this morning if I wanted to
be a bird, I might have given you a different answer.**

基礎技巧提點

1 用於表示「與現在事實相反的假設」，若附屬子句為
be 動詞文法時，不論人稱，一律用「were」。文法結
構為：If＋**過去式附屬子句（主詞＋were＋～）**＋逗號
（,）＋**主要子句（主詞＋would /could /should/might
＋～）**。

2 用於表示「與過去事實相反的事」，使用的假設句結構
為：If＋**過去完成式附屬子句（主詞＋had pp.＋～）**＋
逗號（,）＋**主要子句（主詞＋would have/should have/
could have/might have＋動詞或 be 動詞的過去分詞
（如關鍵例句搶先看的 given＋～）**。

✏ **試著翻翻看▶** **試著翻畫底線的部分**

❶ 我常常在想，假如我是一隻鳥，就能自由自在地翱翔天際。我會飛到任何我想去的地方，累了就在高山的岩石或樹梢上休息。從天空眺望平地的景色，一定美得令人屏息。

要是這個願望能成真，我可能會先飛到亞馬遜河（the Amazon River）。由於聽說那裡的雨林生態豐富，從小我就希望有朝一日，能夠到雨林探險，而且說不定在那裡，我會遇到很多新的「鳥」朋友呢！❷ 不過要是你今天早上問我想不想當一隻鳥，也許我的答案會有所不同。

❶ _____

_____

_____

❷ _____

_____

_____

✎ 你翻對了嗎？

❶ 我常常在想，假如我是一隻鳥，就能自由自在地翱翔天際。
我會飛到任何我想去的地方，累了就在高山的岩石或樹梢上
休息。

I often think that if I were a bird, I could fly freely in the
sky. I would fly to anywhere I wanted and rest on the
tree tops or on the rocks in the mountains when I was
tired.

| 為什麼這樣翻 1 ⋯⋯⋯⋯⋯⋯⋯⋯⋯⋯⋯⋯⋯⋯⋯⋯⋯⋯⋯⋯⋯⋯⋯

從「假如我是一隻鳥」，可判定是假設句，因為人不可
能是鳥，所以是**表示「與現在事實相反的假設」**，若附屬子
句為 be 動詞文法時，不論人稱，一律用「were」。文法結
構為：

(1) If＋過去式附屬子句（I were a bird）＋英文逗號
（,）

(2) ＋主要子句（I could fly freely in the sky）。

❷ 不過要是你今天早上問我想不想當一隻鳥，也許我的答案會有所不同。

But if you had asked me this morning if I wanted to be a bird, I might have given you a different answer.

| 為什麼這樣翻 2 ⋯⋯⋯⋯⋯⋯⋯⋯⋯⋯⋯⋯⋯⋯⋯⋯⋯⋯⋯⋯

　　從「要是你今天早上問我想不想當一隻鳥」，表示**「與過去事實相反的事」**，事實上，今天早上，你並沒有問我。使用的假設句文法結構為：

(1) If ＋過去完成式附屬子句（you had asked me this morning if I wanted to be a bird）＋英文逗號（,）

(2) ＋主要子句（I might have given you a different answer）。**動詞 give 不規則的動詞三態：「give-gave-given」**。

❶ 我常常在想，假如我是一隻鳥，就能自由自在地翱翔天際。我會飛到任何我想去的地方，累了就在高山的岩石或樹梢上休息。

I often imagine how I could fly freely in the sky if I were a bird. I would fly to anywhere I wanted while resting on the tree tops or on the rocks in the mountains when I was tired.

| 為什麼還能這樣翻 1 ⋯⋯⋯⋯⋯⋯⋯⋯⋯⋯⋯⋯⋯⋯⋯⋯⋯⋯⋯

這句為假設句，表示**「與現在事實相反的假設」**。可將假設句中，附屬子句與主要子句的位置對換，文法結構為：主要子句（I often imagine how I could fly freely in the sky）＋if＋過去式附屬子句（I were a bird）。

❷ 不過要是你今天早上問我想不想當一隻鳥，也許我的答案會有所不同。

Had you asked me this morning if I wanted to be a bird, I might have given you a different answer.

│ 為什麼還能這樣翻 2 ⋯⋯⋯⋯⋯⋯⋯⋯⋯⋯⋯⋯⋯⋯⋯⋯⋯⋯⋯⋯

這句也為假設句，表示**「與過去事實相反的事」**。本句

「If you had asked me ...」，亦可寫作「Had you asked

me...」。If +S +had + p.p 等於 Had +S +p.p。

全文翻譯

　　I often think that if I were a bird, I could fly freely in the sky. I would fly to anywhere I wanted and rest on the tree tops or on the rocks in the mountains when I was tired. The view of ground from the sky must be breathtaking.

　　If the dream came true, I might fly to the Amazon River first. Having heard people say it has enriched the rainforest ecosystem, I have hoped one day I could go and explore the rainforest since I was a kid. Perhaps I might meet a lot of new 'bird' friends there! But if you had asked me this morning if I wanted to be a bird, I might have given you a different answer.

「希望」翻成「hope」還是「wish」?

關鍵技巧　端看希望的事情是否有可能成真 ▶

關鍵例句搶先看 ●

到時候,我希望能夠在學校附近租房子,這樣我就能養寵物。

By that time I hope that I can rent a house near my school, so I can have pets.

基礎技巧提點

1 英文標點符號不需與中文標點符號配合,通常一段句子中,最多不超過兩個逗號或分號,就必須下句號、問號、驚嘆號,做為完整語意結束。

2 從中文語意辨讀每個句子的各別時態。

3 中文標點符號,圓括號「( )」用於標註插入語或修飾評論。

4 適時加入連接詞、形容詞子句,讓譯文更流暢通順。

5 了解中文語意後,再譯成英文,配合英語語法。不逐字譯。

✐ 試著翻翻看 ▶ 試著翻畫底線的部分

❶ 一位朋友告訴我，說她期待每天下課後，帶著她最心愛的馬爾濟斯犬（Maltese Dog）——「小白」，到公園散步。

小時候，父母不准我養寵物，我認為他們應該是覺得這樣家裡會不乾淨，或是嫌麻煩。❷ 現在我已經高中三年級，即將在今年暑假讀大學，到時候，我希望能夠在學校附近租房子，這樣我就能養寵物。

❶ _____

_____

_____

❷ _____

_____

_____

❶ 一位朋友告訴我，說她期待每天下課後，帶著她最心愛的馬爾濟斯犬（Maltese Dog）──「小白」，到公園散步。

One of my friends told me that every day she looks forward to going home after school, so she can walk her dearest Maltese Dog-"Little White" in the park.

| 為什麼這樣翻 1 ···

　　「一位朋友告訴我」，是過去式，並注意這句就是「我的很多朋友中的其中一位」的意思。「帶著她最心愛的馬爾濟斯犬（Maltese Dog）──「小白」，到公園散步」，**帶狗散步即是「溜狗」的意思，英文是「walk（someone's）dog」**。

　　適時加入並列連接詞「, so」＋主要子句，讓語意更完整，不會在「after school」後就以句點斷句。

❷ 現在我已經高中三年級，即將在今年暑假讀大學，到時候，我希望能夠在學校附近租房子，這樣我就能養寵物。

Now I am in my junior year of high school and will go to university this summer. By that time I hope that I can rent a house near my school, so I can have pets.

│ 為什麼這樣翻 2 ⋯⋯⋯⋯⋯⋯⋯⋯⋯⋯⋯⋯⋯⋯⋯⋯⋯⋯⋯⋯⋯

　　「即將在今年暑假讀大學」，是未來式文法。「hope + that ...」表示期望有可能成真的事，不可翻成 wish，因為 wish 所希望的事較不可能成真，和此句的原意不符。

　　「養寵物」是「have pets」，**請注意名詞的單複數**。英文語序將地方和時間放在句尾，如：in my junior year of high school、this summer；時間副詞也可以放在主詞前，如 this summer、By this time。時間副詞後加英文逗號與否皆可。

❶ 一位朋友告訴我，說她期待每天下課後，帶著她最心愛的馬爾濟斯犬（Maltese Dog）——「小白」，到公園散步。

One of my friends told me that every day she expects after school the most, so she can take her darling dog which is a Maltese Dog named "Little White" to the park.

| 為什麼還能這樣翻 1 ···

　　「期待」亦可以「expect」表示，本句為現在式，故第三人稱動詞要加「s」。另外，可用形容詞子句的補充敘述，代替破折號（——）。關係代名詞「which」用來表示在它之前的名詞（事／物）。狗的名字是主人取的，在英文語法中需使用被動語態，**被動的文法架構為：主詞＋be 動詞＋過去分詞**（name－named－named）。由於 Maltese Dog 為原附屬子句的受詞，因此可以省略 which 和 be 動詞。省略前的句子會是「which is named "Little White"」。

❷ 現在我已經高中三年級，即將在今年暑假讀大學，到時候，我希望能夠在學校附近租房子，這樣我就能養寵物。

I am a third-grade high school student now. I will be going to university this summer, and I hope by that time

I can rent a house near my school. In that case, I can have pets.

| 為什麼還能這樣翻 2

「高中三年級」亦可譯作「a third-grade high school student」。「**即將在今年暑假讀大學**」是**未來式文法**。「going to」是「即將」的意思，是片語。「這樣我就能養寵物」的前一句譯文已以句號做為結束，因此以「In that case」片語作為另一個完整句子的開頭，意思是「如此一來，我便能養寵物」，並不影響原意。

全文翻譯

One of my friends told me that every day she looks forward to going home after school, so she can walk her dearest Maltese Dog－ "Little White" in the park.

When I was a kid, my parents wouldn't allow me to have any pets. I think that's because they might think it will not be easy to keep the house clean while having pets, or they just simply wanted to save the trouble. Now I am in my junior year of high school and will go to university this summer. By that time I hope that I can rent a house near my school, so I can have pets.

搞懂英文的「直接引述」、「間接引述」；還有引述內容的時態也很重要！ ▶

關鍵例句搶先看 ◉

醫生告訴我：「你得了乳癌。檢查的結果顯示為第一期乳癌。」

My doctor told me, "You have breast cancer. The results show that you have first stage breast cancer."

基礎技巧提點

1 醫療術語的固有譯文，皆需查證。

2 敘述已發生的事件時，通常用「過去式」、「完成式」、「過去進行式」。

3 直接引述的內容，時態為當時的情境，多為現在式，但仍視內文而定。

4 英文譯文的寫法需符合時態、詞性、語法，一句話常能有多種表達方式，但所傳達的意思與文法，必須準確無誤。

✎ 試著翻翻看▶ 試著翻畫底線的部分

　　二年前，在我五十九歲的那一年，**❶** 醫生告訴我：「你得了乳癌。檢查的結果顯示為第一期乳癌。」在聽到醫生宣判病情的當下，我的思緒一片空白，腦海裡有個聲音不斷重播著：「為什麼是我？」，但我仍忍住激動不安的情緒，仔細聆聽醫生的解說，**❷** 他告訴我，由於我每年都定期做身體檢查，才能幸運地及早發現罹患乳癌，及早治療。

　　第一期乳癌的治癒率近百分之百。現在我已經康復，也持續不斷鼓勵身邊的人，定期做身體檢查。

❶ _____

_____

_____

❷ _____

_____

_____

❶ 醫生告訴我：「你得了乳癌。檢查的結果顯示為第一期乳癌。」

..., my doctor told me, "You have breast cancer. The results show that you have first stage breast cancer."

| 為什麼這樣翻 1 ....

　　本句為直接引述，即直接錄自說話者所說的內容。英文的標點符號以「 "" 」表示某人說話的內容；句中用於表達主詞的代名詞，與間接引述的說法，會有所不同。「你得了乳癌。檢查的結果顯示為第一期乳癌。」這句採直接引述，引述內容的代名詞主詞為「你」（you）。

❷ 他告訴我，由於我每年都定期做身體檢查，才能幸運地及早發現罹患乳癌，及早治療。

He told me that because of regularly doing health examinations, I am lucky to find out that I have breast cancer early enough to treat it.

| 為什麼這樣翻 2 ⋯⋯⋯⋯⋯⋯⋯⋯⋯⋯⋯⋯⋯⋯⋯⋯⋯⋯⋯⋯⋯⋯

　　本句為間接引述，是間接地報告出某人的話，因此句中主詞的代名詞表達，會有所不同，其引述中的代名詞主詞為「我」（I）。

　　「及早發現罹患乳癌，及早治療」，**在符合英文語法的情況下，即為「及早發現（某事）來得及治療」，以「副詞（early）＋副詞（enough）＋to ＋動詞（原形，也就是treat）＋代名詞受詞** it（**表示** breast cancer）」譯出。

❶ 醫生告訴我：「你得了乳癌。檢查的結果顯示為第一期乳癌。」

...,my doctor informed me, "You have developed breast cancer. According to the results, you have first stage breast cancer."

| 為什麼還能這樣翻 1 ···

　　「你得了乳癌」，在病理上，較專業的說法，是以「發展－develop」來表示一種疾病的產生，或經診斷出罹患某種疾病的狀態。

❷ 他告訴我，由於我每年都定期做身體檢查，才能幸運地及早發現罹患乳癌，及早治療。

He said to me, "Because you do health examinations regularly, fortunately it has been found at an early enough stage for treatment."

| 為什麼還能這樣翻 2 ···

　　本句由**間接引述的代名詞主詞（I）**，變成**直接引述代名詞主詞（you）**。「及早發現罹患乳癌，及早治療」，亦

以**過去完成式的被動語態**譯出，其文法結構為：**主詞（it）＋has＋be 動詞的過去分詞（been）＋過去分詞（found）**；「發現」動詞三態 ―「find-found-found」。

全文翻譯

Two years ago, when I was fifty-nine, my doctor told me, "You have breast cancer. The results show that you have first stage breast cancer." The moment I heard my doctor announce my condition, my mind went blank, and there was a sound in my head, it kept repeating, "Why me?" I somehow restrained my emotionally disturbed feelings and listened closely to the doctor's explanation of my conditions. He told me that because of regularly doing health examinations, I am lucky to find out that I have breast cancer early enough to treat it.

The cure rate of first stage breast cancer is nearly a hundred percent. I am fully recovered now, and keep encouraging everyone around me to do their health examinations regularly.

什麼時候加「an」、
什麼時候加「the」？

關鍵技巧　搞懂冠詞－不定冠詞、定冠詞的用法！ ▶

關鍵例句搶先看 ●

在十九歲之前，我並沒有出國的經驗，很幸運地是，去年我到澳洲當了一年的交換學生。

I hadn't been abroad before I was nineteen; then luckily, I went to Australia as an exchange student last year.

基礎技巧提點

1 定冠詞「the」，可與單、複數名詞連用，亦可用於表示特定的不可數名詞；若不可數名詞為非特定性質時，則不需加冠詞。最高級以「est」結尾的形容詞之前，必需加定冠詞。

2 **「專有名詞」、「國家名」不可與冠詞連用。**

3 名詞之前有所有格修飾時，不可再使用冠詞。如：my book。

4 不定冠詞「a／an」，是指非特定東西，只與單數名詞連字。

✎ 試著翻翻看▶ **試著翻畫底線的部分**

我在印度長大，最大的夢想就是出國旅行。**❶** 在十九歲之前，我並沒有出國的經驗，很幸運地是，去年我到澳洲當了一年的交換學生，這是我生平第一次出國的體驗，而我也因此愛上澳洲。

去年四月，我造訪澳洲其中一處最著名的地標－雪梨歌劇院（Sydney Opera House），我很享受在那裡觀賞節目的感覺，我認為，它是我看過最美妙的劇院！**❷** 雖然現在我已經回到印度，繼續完成我的大學學業，但是在澳洲的美好回憶，仍舊十分鮮明。我期待畢業後，能夠到澳洲工作。

❶ _____

_____

_____

❷ _____

_____

_____

❶ 在十九歲之前，我並沒有出國的經驗，很幸運地是，去年我到澳洲當了一年的交換學生。

I hadn't been abroad before I was nineteen; then luckily, I went to Australia as an exchange student last year.

| 為什麼這樣翻 1 ⋯⋯⋯⋯⋯⋯⋯⋯⋯⋯⋯⋯⋯⋯⋯⋯⋯⋯⋯

「我並沒有出國的經驗」，使用「have been」表示「去過」；而「have gone」則是表示「去了（現在還沒回來）」。

「去年我到澳洲當了一年的交換學生」，名詞片語「an exchange student（交換學生）」，配合前文主詞「I（我）」，其單數名詞要加不定冠詞「a」，這裡要用「an」，對應 exchange 該字的母音字首（e）。「Australia」是國家名，不可加冠詞。

❷ 雖然現在我已經回到印度，繼續完成我的大學學業，但是在澳洲的美好回憶，仍舊十分鮮明。

Although I am back to India now continuing my university education, the wonderful memories of Australia are still vividly remembered.

| 為什麼這樣翻 2 ⋯⋯⋯⋯⋯⋯⋯⋯⋯⋯⋯⋯⋯⋯⋯⋯⋯⋯⋯

可數名詞複數形式「memories」，為特定用意，需加上定冠詞「the」。

「雖然……，但是……」此句的文法結構為：從屬連接詞（although）＋從屬子句（I am back to India now continuing my university education）＋英文逗號（,）＋ 主要子句 （現在式被動語態－主詞（the wonderful memories of Australia））＋be 動詞（are）＋副詞（still）＋副詞（vividly）＋過去分詞（remembered））。

❶ 在十九歲之前，我並沒有出國的經驗，很幸運地是，去年我到澳洲當了一年的交換學生。

Before I was lucky enough to visit Australia as a nineteen-year-old exchange student last year, I had never been abroad.

| 為什麼還能這樣翻 1 ···

此句亦可寫作從屬連接詞（before）＋從屬子句（I was lucky enough to visit Australia... last year）＋英文逗號（,）＋ 主要子句 （I had never been abroad）。

❷ 雖然現在我已經回到印度，繼續完成我的大學學業，但是在澳洲的美好回憶，仍舊十分鮮明。

My wonderful Australian memories are still vivid in my mind as I now continue my university education back in India.

| 為什麼還能這樣翻 2 ···

依其語意，亦可將主要子句放在前面，譯作： 主要子句 （my wonderful Australian memories are... mind）＋從屬連

接詞（as）＋從屬子句（I now continue my university education back in India.）。「澳洲的美好回憶」，其「澳洲」亦可譯作形容詞形式「Australian」，來修飾可數複數名詞「memories」。

全文翻譯

I grew up in India, and the greatest dream of mine was to travel abroad. I hadn't been abroad before I was nineteen; then luckily, I went to Australia as an exchange student last year. This was my first experience of being abroad, and because of that, I have fallen in love with Australia.

Last April, I visited one of the most famous landmarks in Australia-Sydney Opera House. I enjoyed watching a show in it, and I think it is the most amazing theater I have ever seen. Although I am back to India now continuing my university education, the wonderful memories of Australia are still vividly remembered. I look forward to working in Australia after I finished my degree.

2-1 英文的比較級怎麼用？

關鍵
技巧 **記住副詞和形容詞的變化規則！** ▶

關鍵例句搶先看 ◉

今年夏季氣溫，預期比往年高出攝氏兩度，因此防曬也變得不可或缺。

Temperatures this summer time are predicted to be 2°C higher than usual; therefore, guarding against the sun has become necessary.

基礎技巧提點

1 表示溫度的單位及數值，皆以符號與阿拉伯數字譯出。

2 **中文語法有「比；愈；更；最」，即是用到英文裡的比較級與最高級。**

3 形容詞單音節的比較級／最高級，在字尾加上「er／est」。在最高級的 est 前要加「the」

4 形容詞是兩個或更多音節的形容詞，以及副詞的比較級／最高級，是於原形形容詞前面，加上「more/the most」；但有些形容詞和副詞的比較級是不規則的。

5 看完整個句子、段落，再下筆，譯意不譯字。

✒️ **試著翻翻看▶** **試著翻畫底線的部分**

❶ 今年夏季氣溫，預期比往年高出攝氏兩度，因此防曬也變得不可或缺。不僅要多補充水份，也不宜暴露在陽光下過久。

近年來，全球氣候變得愈漸極端化，世界各國不得不執行減少碳排放量的行動，希望能減緩全球暖化的速度。一般民眾能就日常生活消費習慣的改變，實踐減少碳排放量：❷ 減少免洗餐具的使用，不購買過度包裝的商品。讓我們一同創造更美好的世界！

❶ _____

_____

_____

❷ _____

_____

_____

❶ 今年夏季氣溫，預期比往年高出攝氏兩度，因此防曬也變得不可或缺。

Temperatures this summer time are predicted to be 2℃ higher than usual; therefore, guarding against the sun has become necessary.

| 為什麼這樣翻 1 ⋯⋯⋯⋯⋯⋯⋯⋯⋯⋯⋯⋯⋯⋯⋯⋯

中文的「不可或缺」，也就是「必需」的意思。

比較級通常與「than」連用，「今年夏季氣溫，預期比往年高出攝氏兩度」，**這個「高」是形容詞**，修飾名詞「氣溫」，因此比較級為「higher」；**若是作副詞用**，則是不規則的比較級「較高地-high-high」。

❷ 減少免洗餐具的使用，不購買過度包裝的商品。讓我們一同
創造更美好的世界！

...: reducing the frequency of using disposable cutlery
and not purchasing excessively packed products. Let us
build a better world together!

| 為什麼這樣翻 2

　　本段全以現在式表示，為敘述常態事項，未有特定的時
間背景。「減少免洗餐具的使用」，在全文中是在冒號之
後，有表示系列的意思，不需大寫。**現在分詞當主詞
（reducing, purchasing），表示主動。唯需注意介系詞
「of」後必須是名詞，因此動詞需加「ing」變成動名詞
（動名詞是名詞）。**「更美好的」是形容詞，修飾名詞「世
界」，比較級為不規則變化，為「good-better」。

❶ 今年夏季氣溫，預期比往年高出攝氏兩度，因此防曬也變得不可或缺。

It is forecast that this year's summer time temperatures will be 2℃ higher than usual; therefore, guarding against the sun has become necessary.

| 為什麼還能這樣翻 1 ⋯⋯⋯⋯⋯⋯⋯⋯⋯⋯⋯⋯⋯⋯⋯⋯⋯⋯⋯⋯⋯⋯

　　依中文語意，亦可理解為「預報顯示今年夏季氣溫將比往年高出攝氏兩度」，並以此翻成英文。第一個子句為被動語態：主詞＋be 動詞＋過去分詞（過去式和過去分詞寫作 forecast 或 forecasted 皆可）；**用關係代名詞「that」領導形容詞子句，指「It is forecast」這件事。**

❷ 減少免洗餐具的使用，不購買過度包裝的商品。讓我們一同創造更美好的世界！

...: reducing the frequency of using disposable cutlery and not purchasing excessively packed products. Together, we can build a better world!

| 為什麼還能這樣翻 2 ··········

　　「過度包裝的商品」，其「過度」要寫成副詞形式－「excessively」，修飾形容詞「包裝的」－「packed」。副詞（together）可放在主詞（we）之前，但需在副詞後加逗號。

　　Temperatures this summer time are predicted to be 2˚C higher than usual; therefore, guarding against the sun has become necessary. Not only drink more fluid, but also avoid direct exposure to the sun.

　　In the past few years, the world's weather has become more and more extreme. Every country around the world has been forced into the action to reduce carbon emissions, in the hope of slowing down global warming. The public can put it into practice by changing daily consumption habits: reducing the frequency of using disposable cutlery and not purchasing excessively packed products. Let us build a better world together!

2-2 所有格怎麼用？

關鍵
技巧 **學會名詞所有格的變化！** ▶

關鍵例句搶先看 ▶

萊拉的母親是位專業的蒙特梭利三至六歲幼教老師

Lyla's mother is a Montessori teacher who specializes in children's education between the age of three and six.

基礎技巧提點

1 「六歲生日」，的英文譯法，需寫作「第六個生日」。

2 名詞的所有格，若是非「s」結尾的名詞，直接在字尾加上高逗點（'）和「s」。如：Lyla's。

3 名詞的所有格，若是單數並以「s」結尾的名詞，則加上高逗點（'）和「s」。如：boss's。

4 名詞的所有格，若是複數並以「s」結尾的名詞，直接在字尾「s」加上高逗點（'）。如：employees'。

5 看完整個句子、段落，再下筆。

✎ 試著翻翻看▶ **試著翻畫底線的部分**

　　萊拉（Lyla）是個善良又率直的六歲女孩。她的堅強個性，有助她有自信地面對生活中的種種挑戰。❶ 萊拉的母親是位專業的蒙特梭利三至六歲幼教老師，父親從事製造業技師工作，他們最喜歡跟萊拉一同創作。

　　今年六月，萊拉即將慶祝她的六歲生日。❷ 我已經先到百貨公司的兒童樓層，買了她最喜歡的恐龍布偶，作為她的生日禮物。希望她會喜歡。

❶ _____

_____

_____

❷ _____

_____

_____

❶ 萊拉的母親是位專業的蒙特梭利三至六歲幼教老師。

Lyla's mother is a Montessori teacher who specializes in children's education between the age of three and six.

| 為什麼這樣翻 1 ···

　　名詞的所有格，若是非「s」結尾的名詞，直接在字尾加上高逗點（'）和「s」。「萊拉的」，譯作「Lyla's」。「幼教」，譯作「children's education」。「三至六歲」表示兩個數值之間的值，在英文中使用「between... and...」。

❷ 我已經先到百貨公司的兒童樓層，買了她最喜歡的恐龍布偶，作為她的生日禮物。

I have already been to the department store's children's floor, and bought her favorite dinosaur puppet as the birthday present for her.

| 為什麼這樣翻 2 ⋯⋯⋯⋯⋯⋯⋯⋯

「我已經先到」，表示「已經去過並回來了」，英文語法使用「have been」。「百貨公司的兒童樓層」，英文需以所有格表示，即「department store's children's floor」；名詞－「兒童」的單複數為不規則「a child－children」，變為所有格時要於名詞「children」後加高逗點（'）和「s」。

「作為她的生日禮物」，意即「我給她的生日禮物」，先翻生日禮物「the birthday present」，給她則翻成「for her」，這句成為「the birthday present for her」，來形容恐龍布偶，也就是禮物本身，等同「the birthday present」，前面放入「as」（中文意為：有如；作為）的介系詞，連結「dinosaur puppet」和「the birthday present for her」。

❶ 萊拉的母親是位專業的蒙特梭利三至六歲幼教老師。

Lyla's mother is a Montessori teacher specializing in the education of children three to six years old.

| 為什麼還能這樣翻 1 ·····················

　　「專業的蒙特梭利三至六歲幼教老師」，亦可省略表示受詞的關係代名詞「who」，**以現在分詞（specializing）當作為形容詞子句的主詞**。「三至六歲」，亦可譯作「three to six years old」。

❷ 我已經先到百貨公司的兒童樓層，買了她最喜歡的恐龍布偶，作為她的生日禮物。

I went to the department store's children's floor, and bought her favorite dinosaur puppet as the birthday present for her.

| 為什麼還能這樣翻 2 ·····················

　　「我已經先到百貨公司的兒童樓層」，亦可用過去式文法表示，使用過去式動詞「去－go－went」；並列連接詞（,and）連接的第二個主要子句時態，需配合第一個主要子

句，皆使用過去式，使用過去式動詞「買－buy－bought」。

全文翻譯

Lyla is a straightforward and kind hearted six-year-old girl. Her strong character helps her face all the challenges of life with confidence. Lyla's mother is a Montessori teacher who specializes in children's education between the age of three and six, and her father is a manufacturing technician. Both of them like nothing more than making things with Lyla.

Lyla will be celebrating her sixth birthday in June. I have already been to the department store's children's floor, and bought her favorite dinosaur puppet as the birthday present for her. I hope she will like it.

2-3 副詞怎麼用？

搞懂副詞用法 ▶

關鍵例句搶先看 ◉

我清楚地記得，第一次帶我兒子到海灘的情景。

I clearly remember the first time I took my son to the beach.

基礎技巧提點

1 副詞用於修飾動詞、副詞、形容詞，和整個句子。規則的形容詞變副詞形式，在字尾加「ly」；若字尾為「子音＋y」，則刪除「y」再加上「ily」。如：clearly；easily。

2 「late」在英文中有兩種不同的意思，一是指「晚的；晚期的」，另一指「已故的」。

3 「春末夏初」，即為「late spring」或「the beginning of summer」，但兩者不能同時出現，因為這兩種說法代表同一個時間點。

✏️ 試著翻翻看 ▶ **試著翻畫底線的部分**

❶ <u>我清楚地記得，第一次帶我兒子到海灘的情景。</u>一個春末夏初的大熱天，我們在墾丁（Kenting），當時我的兒子約十八個月大。

❷ <u>他在看見閃閃發亮的沙子時，立即緊緊地抱著我，不讓我放他下來。</u>鼓勵他一番之後，在找到勇氣自己踩在沙子上之前，他開始慢慢地用腳趾感受沙子。

最後，他那天花了幾小時，開心地玩沙子。可是他都沒有走遠，一直留在距離我幾英吋的地方。

❶ _____

_____

_____

❷ _____

_____

_____

❶ 我清楚地記得，第一次帶我兒子到海灘的情景。

I clearly remember the first time I took my son to the beach.

| 為什麼這樣翻 1 ⋯⋯⋯⋯⋯⋯⋯⋯⋯⋯⋯⋯⋯⋯⋯⋯⋯⋯⋯

　　表狀態的副詞（clearly）修飾動詞（remember），說明「如何」做某事。規則的形容詞（clear）變副詞形式，在字尾加「ly」。

　　雖然中文原文有「情景」一詞，但在通暢的英文譯文中，「clearly remember」即代表清楚記得的，**是接下來要說的「第一次帶我兒子到海灘」的過程，譯其意，不譯其字。不需譯出「情景」一詞。**

❷ 他在看見閃閃發亮的沙子時，立即緊緊地抱著我，不讓我放他下來。

Upon seeing the shiny sand, he held on tightly to me and refused to be put down.

| 為什麼這樣翻 2 ··

「upon」是「在做某件事……立即」，為介系詞，後面一定是名詞；動詞「看見」加「ing」變成動名詞（seeing）。

用於形容「沙子」在視覺上給人的感受，通常以「shiny」表示。副詞（tightly）修飾過去式動詞（held）。「不讓我放他下來」，依前句主詞是「he」，**「不讓」這裡譯為：「refused to」，後面則以「被動語態」表示；** refused to do something 為固定用法，因此 to 後要接原形 be 動詞＋過去分詞（put＋副詞（down））。

❶ 我清楚地記得，第一次帶我兒子到海灘的情景。

I clearly remember the first time I took my son to the beach, as if it were yesterday.

| 為什麼還能這樣翻 1 ···

　　根據原文語意，亦可譯作「我記得第一次帶我兒子到海灘的情景，**猶如**一切昨天才發生般地清晰」。**「猶如」整個句子翻作：「as if it were yesterday」，為表示與現在事實相反的假設句**。本附屬子句 be 動詞文法，因此不論人稱一律用「were」。

❷ 他在看見閃閃發亮的沙子時，立即緊緊地抱著我，不讓我放他下來。

When he saw the shiny sand, he refused to be put down and held on tightly to me.

| 為什麼還能這樣翻 2 ···

　　「立即緊緊地抱著我，不讓我放他下來」是以並列連接詞「and」連接的兩個主要子句（he refused to be put down），因此變成：（【省略主詞 he】）held on tightly to me）。在英文語法中，並列子句中兩個主要子句的先後順序，並不影響語意，但需留意其時態有一致性。

I clearly remember the first time I took my son to the beach. It was a hot day in late spring. We were in Kenting and my son was about eighteen months old.

Upon seeing the shiny sand, he held on tightly to me and refused to be put down. After much encouragement, he slowly began to feel the sand with his toes before finally finding the courage to stand up in it on his own.

In the end, he spent a couple of hours happily playing in the sand that day, but he never moved more than a few feet from my side.

2-4 as... as 怎麼用？

as... as 使用技巧 ▶

關鍵例句搶先看 ◉

英國年青人不再像以前喝那麼多酒，但是那些仍舊如此的人，愈來愈多是在自家飲酒。

The youth of Britain aren't drinking as much as they used to, and those that do are increasingly doing so at home.

基礎技巧提點

1 「跟……一樣；像……一樣」，在英文文法中以「as…as」表示，用於表達兩者相比較後，相等的狀態，與形容詞或副詞連用，可用於肯定或否定的語意中。

2 副詞修飾動詞、副詞、形容詞、整個句子。

3 「十年」有特定英文用字「a decade」；四分之一有特定英文用字「a quarter」。

4 「營業至凌晨」，在英文中是以形容詞「late-opening」表示。

✏️ **試著翻翻看▶** **試著翻畫底線的部分**

❶ 英國年青人不再像以前喝那麼多酒，但是那些仍舊如此的人，愈來愈多是在自家飲酒。年齡二十五歲以下，五人之中就有一人滴酒不沾。自本世紀初，啤酒銷量下滑超過四分之一，這也不意外，過去十年來，英國已有近半數的夜總會歇業。

❷ 許多愛喝酒的人，不再視夜總會為好的晚上外出小酌的最終場所。他們大概會在家裡待到深夜，前往營業至凌晨的酒吧小酌，然後再返家。

❶ _____

_____

_____

_____

❷ _____

_____

_____

_____

❶ 英國年青人不再像以前喝那麼多酒，但是那些仍舊如此的人，愈來愈多是在自家飲酒。

The youth of Britain aren't drinking as much as they used to, and those that do are increasingly doing so at home.

| 為什麼這樣翻 1 ⋯⋯⋯⋯⋯⋯⋯⋯⋯⋯⋯⋯⋯⋯⋯⋯⋯⋯⋯⋯⋯⋯

　　本句為現在式文法。「英國年青人不再像以前喝那麼多酒」，表示以前是喝很多酒，但是現在不再如此，文法以「used to」表示；酒是不可數名詞，用「as much（副詞）as」表示。

　　「愈來愈多是在自家飲酒」此句的主詞亦是指「英國年青人」，但為避免重複，**因此以「those」代稱，後接關係代名詞「that」形容「those」**，整句翻成「those that do are increasingly doing so at home.」，「increasingly」（副詞），修飾動詞「do」（指 drink，這個動詞前句已出現過，因此改為 do）。

❷ 許多愛喝酒的人，不再視夜總會為好的晚上外出小酌的最終場所。

Many drinkers no longer see nightclubs as the final destination of a good night out.

| 為什麼這樣翻 2 ....

　　「視……為」，英文以「see... as...」表示。「許多愛喝酒的人」，在英文以可數名詞「drinker」表示，故用與可數名詞複數連用的「many」，並在可數名詞字尾加「s」。

　　「好的晚上外出（做某件事；通常指休閒活動）」看起來很像是動詞，但仔細看是指「外出場所」，英文以「a good night out」，名詞表示。

❶ 英國年青人不再像以前喝那麼多酒，但是那些仍舊如此的人，愈來愈多是在自家飲酒。

British youths don't drink as much alcohol as before, and when they do, it is done often at home.

| 為什麼還能這樣翻 1 ⋯⋯⋯⋯⋯⋯⋯⋯⋯⋯⋯⋯⋯⋯⋯⋯⋯⋯⋯⋯⋯⋯⋯⋯⋯⋯

「喝酒」也能寫作「drink alcohol」，但是通常以「drink」即為明確表示喝酒的意思。「much」與不可數名詞連用，而「alcohol」酒精為不可數名詞。「喝那麼多酒」的這件事，常是在自家發生，使用現在式動詞的被動語態，表示這件事是被英國年青人做了的。

❷ 許多愛喝酒的人，不再視夜總會為好的晚上外出小酌的最終場所。

The nightclub has fallen out of favor as the final step of a good night out for those that drink.

| 為什麼還能這樣翻 2 ⋯⋯⋯⋯⋯⋯⋯⋯⋯⋯⋯⋯⋯⋯⋯⋯⋯⋯⋯⋯⋯⋯⋯⋯⋯⋯⋯

「不再視夜總會為好的⋯⋯」翻為「fallen out of favor」，表示「失寵」的意思。是因為「誰」而失寵？亦即「許多愛

喝酒的人」，因此「fallen out of favor」後要加「介系詞
（for）＋主詞（those）＋關係代名詞（that）＋不及物動
詞（drink）」。

全文翻譯

The youth of Britain aren't drinking as much as they
used to, and those that do are increasingly doing so at
home. With one in five under-25-year-olds teetotal and
beer sales down more than a quarter since the turn of
the century, it is little wonder that almost half of the
UK's nightclubs have closed in the last decade.

Many drinkers no longer see nightclubs as the final
destination of a good night out. They are likely to stay
home until late in the evening, visit a late-opening bar
and then return home.

3-1 中文沒有過去式、現在完成式，英文可不能沒有！

關鍵技巧 過去式、現在完成式用法 ▶

關鍵例句搶先看 ▶

我每天騎機車上班，可是就在昨天，我買了人生中的第一部車子。

I ride a scooter to work every day, but yesterday I bought my first car.

基礎技巧提點

1 從中文語意辨讀時態，或依段落陳述的時間點與情境辨別時態。

2 在不影響語意的情況下，可適時簡化或加入譯出文，讓譯文更完整通順。

3 詞性的規則，介系詞後面一定是名詞。

4 專有名詞譯法需查證，已固有的譯名譯出。

5 英文的標點符號，破折號「─」用於介紹某種說法，加入強調語氣、定義或解釋。

✏️ 試著翻翻看▶ 試著翻畫底線的部分

❶ <u>我每天騎機車上班</u>，可是就在昨天，<u>我買了人生中的第一部車子</u>。我已經存了好久的錢，終於可以買我最喜歡的奧迪（Audi）。為了慶祝買新車，朋友還替我籌劃一個派對，下個星期五，我跟朋友一行共五人，將前往露營場地度過周末。

❷ <u>雖然買了車子，不過我還是決定騎機車上班</u>，因為我上班的地方，附近停車位不好找。既然有了車子，我便打算每個週末都開車去不同的地方玩。我愛我的新車。

❶ _____

_____

_____

❷ _____

_____

_____

❶ 我每天騎機車上班，可是就在昨天，我買了人生中的第一部車子。

I ride a scooter to work every day, but yesterday I bought my first car.

| 為什麼這樣翻 1 ⋯⋯⋯⋯⋯⋯⋯⋯⋯⋯⋯⋯⋯⋯⋯⋯⋯⋯⋯⋯⋯⋯⋯⋯⋯⋯⋯⋯⋯

「我每天騎機車上班」是現在式文法；下一個句子點出「昨天」，因此後面的敘述，「買了人生中的第一部車子」則是過去式文法。

要注意不要犯最基礎的錯誤──名詞的單數、複數。**若是單數可數名詞，則要加冠詞「a」。**

❷ 雖然買了車子，不過我還是決定騎機車上班，因為我上班的
地方，附近停車位不好找。

Although I have bought a car, I have still decided to ride
a scooter to work because it's not easy to find a parking
space near where I work.

| 為什麼這樣翻 2 ·······························

　　「雖然買了車子」，中文裡是敘述已完成的事，翻成英
文要使用現在完成式。「不過我還是決定騎機車上班」，意
指當時就決定，**且這個決定將會維持一段時間，因此要用現
在完成式文法**。「因為我上班的地方附近停車位不好找」為
敘述常態事件，是現在式文法。

❶ 我每天騎機車上班，可是就在昨天，我買了人生中的第一部車子。

Every day, I ride a scooter to work, but yesterday, I bought my first car.

| 為什麼還能這樣翻 1 ⋯⋯⋯⋯⋯⋯⋯⋯⋯⋯⋯⋯⋯⋯⋯⋯⋯⋯⋯⋯

　　時間副詞置於主詞前時，需在時間副詞後加上逗號。依本句前後文的中文語意，時間副詞（every day、yesterday）可放在主詞前或在地方與時間的後面。

❷ 雖然買了車子，不過我還是決定騎機車上班，因為我上班的地方，附近停車位不好找。

Despite buying a car, I have still decided to ride a scooter to work since it is not easy to find parking spaces near where I work.

| 為什麼還能這樣翻 2 ⋯⋯⋯⋯⋯⋯⋯⋯⋯⋯⋯⋯⋯⋯⋯⋯⋯⋯⋯⋯

　　不要逐句、逐字照順序譯出，要符合語意與英文文法。「despite」是介系詞，後面必須加名詞；若後面為動詞則

必須加 ing 變成動名詞。「since」由於；因為，是從屬連接
詞，用於連接兩個子句（主要子句和從屬子句）。

I ride a scooter to work every day, but yesterday I bought my first car. I have been saving money for a long time, and finally I could buy my favorite make of car-Audi. In order to celebrate that I bought a new car, my friends organized a party for me. Next Friday, there will be five of us going to a camping site for the weekend.

Although I have bought a car, I have still decided to ride a scooter to work because it's not easy to find a parking space near where I work. Since I have a car now, I intend to drive everywhere and visit different places every weekend. I love my new car.

咦？中文裡明明沒有提到被動式啊，為什麼英文裡有呢？

關鍵技巧　善用英文被動式 ▶

關鍵例句搶先看 ◎

各部門主管應於一月十六日（下星期五），上午九時，至 M 飯店會議廳開會。

A meeting will be held on Jan 16th (next Friday) at 9am at the conference hall in M Hotel. All department heads are required to attend.

基礎技巧提點

1 從中文語意辨讀每個句子的各別時態，注意動詞與 be 動詞在不同時態下的變化。

2 **中文不易在文字中看出英語語法的被動語態，翻譯時需符合英文語法。**

3 看完整個句子、段落，了解其意後再譯出，譯意不譯字。

4 中文標點符號「（　）」表示標註插入語或修飾評論。

✎ 試著翻翻看▶ 試著翻畫底線的部分

❶ <u>各部門主管應於一月十六日（下星期五），上午九時，至 M 飯店會議廳開會</u>。此會議將宣佈公司下一季營運目標。務必準時出席。❷ <u>請各主管在會議前與各部門同仁彙整出建議與檢討事項</u>。此內部會議僅資訊科技部門不需參與。

❶ _____

_____

_____

❷ _____

_____

_____

❶ 各部門主管應於一月十六日（下星期五），上午九時，至 M 飯店會議廳開會。

A meeting will be held on Jan 16th (next Friday) at 9am at the conference hall in M Hotel. All department heads are required to attend.

| 為什麼這樣翻 1 ⋯⋯⋯⋯⋯⋯⋯⋯⋯⋯⋯⋯⋯⋯⋯⋯⋯⋯⋯⋯⋯⋯

本句的**中文雖看不出來為被動式，但英文語法可用未來式被動語態來翻**。「會議將在一月十六日（下星期五），上午九時，在 M 飯店舉行。」。主詞（A meeting）＋未來式 be 動詞（will be）＋過去分詞（held）。「舉行」的動詞三態：「hold-held-held」。

「各部門主管應⋯⋯」，中文雖有主動語態，但可理解成「各部門主管皆被要求出席」的意思，是現在式被動語態。主詞（All department heads）＋現在式 be 動詞（are）＋過去分詞（required）。

❷ 請各主管在會議前與各部門同仁彙整出建議與檢討事項。

Before the meeting, please discuss with the personnel in your department about any issues that need to be brought up and discussed.

| 為什麼這樣翻 2 ··

　　祈使句，主詞可省略。

　　「彙整出建議與檢討事項」，轉成英文語法為「需被提出並檢討的事項」，是現在式被動語態。主詞（any issues）＋動詞（need）＋不定詞（to ＋be 動詞的原形動詞）＋過去分詞（brought）。「bring-brought-brought」關係代名詞「that」可在句中當主詞或受詞，作受詞用時可省略。

❶ 各部門主管應於一月十六日（下星期五），上午九時，至 M 飯店會議廳開會。

The head of each department should attend the meeting which will be held at the conference hall in M Hotel on January 16th (next Friday) 9am.

| 為什麼還能這樣翻 1 ⋯⋯⋯⋯⋯⋯⋯⋯⋯⋯⋯⋯⋯⋯⋯⋯⋯⋯⋯⋯⋯⋯⋯⋯⋯⋯⋯⋯⋯⋯

　　首先，第一主詞從事件發生的地點，改為人物應該至……某場所集合。而這個場所是會議「將被」舉行的地點，如此理解後，這句會用到未來式被動語態，句型結構為：主詞（關係代名詞 which）＋未來式 be 動詞（will be）＋過去分詞（held）。關係代名詞「which」領導的形容詞子句，用來代表在它之前的名詞、事物。時間副詞和地方副詞的順序，有時可以互換，不影響其文法及語意。

❷ 請各主管在會議前與各部門同仁彙整出建議與檢討事項。

Please discuss with the personnel in your department about any issues that need to be brought up and discussed before the meeting.

祈使句，主詞可省略。時間片語（before the meeting）可以用在句首或句尾。

A meeting will be held on Jan 16th (next Friday) at 9am at the conference hall in M Hotel. All department heads are required to attend. In the meeting, we will announce our goals for the following season. Please attend the meeting on time. Before the meeting, please discuss with the personnel in your department about any issues that need to be brought up and discussed. Only the Information Technology department doesn't have to attend this internal meeting.

中文的「從來」要如何和英文的「現在完成式」連結？

關鍵技巧 搞懂「現在完成式」，精確描述英文裡的時間長短 ▶

關鍵例句搶先看 ▶

我從來沒看過老師如此生氣地說話：「你們坐好，閉嘴！」

I have never seen my teacher talk so angrily, "Sit up, and shut up!" she said.

基礎技巧提點

1 現在完成式通常指過去非特定時間發生的事（動作），或是用於描述過去具重複性的事（動作）；亦可用於描述過去某個時間發生並持續至現在的事（動作）。

2 先看完整句、整段，再依語意辨定英文語法的時態。

3 祈使句用於表達命令或要求，會省略主詞。

4 注意名詞的單數與複數變化。

5 副詞用於修飾動詞、副詞、形容詞，和整個句子。

6 標點符號與語序須符合英文語法。

✏️ 試著翻翻看▶ **試著翻畫底線的部分**

　　這學期，班上來了一位新的女同學，她紅髮、身型瘦小。正當老師要她做自我介紹時，少數幾個同學卻仍七嘴八舌地說個不停，❶ 我從來沒看過老師如此生氣地說話：「你們坐好，閉嘴！全班都安靜了下來，新同學告訴我們她的母親是台灣人，父親是美國人，❷ 先前住在美國，現在來台灣定居，因此中文說得不是很好，但是台灣對她來說並不陌生。

❶ _____

_____

_____

❷ _____

_____

_____

❶ 我從來沒看過老師如此生氣地說話：「你們坐好，閉嘴！」

I have never seen my teacher talk so angrily, "Sit up, and shut up!" she said.

| 為什麼這樣翻 1 ⋯⋯⋯⋯⋯⋯⋯⋯⋯⋯⋯⋯⋯⋯⋯⋯⋯⋯⋯⋯⋯⋯⋯⋯⋯⋯⋯⋯⋯⋯⋯⋯⋯

　　英文表示某人所說的話，標點符號以「, ""」表示。「我從來沒看過」，**可依語意辨定英文語法的時態，也就是「從以前到現在為止」的一段時間，因此要使用現在完成式**，本句結構為：主詞（I）＋have＋頻率副詞（never）＋過去分詞（seen；動詞三態變化 see-saw-seen）＋受詞（my teacher）＋受詞補語（talk）＋副詞（so angrily）。「如此生氣地說話」，因為「說話」是動詞，所以「生氣」必須用副詞形式：形容詞 angry－副詞 angrily；「如此－so」作副詞用修飾「生氣地」。「你們坐好，閉嘴！」，是祈使句，主詞（you）省略。

❷ 先前住在美國，現在來台灣定居，因此中文說得不是很好。

They lived in America before, and now they live in Taiwan, thus she can't speak Chinese very well.

| 為什麼這樣翻 2 ⋯⋯⋯⋯⋯⋯⋯⋯⋯⋯⋯⋯⋯⋯⋯⋯⋯⋯⋯⋯

「先前住在美國」，描述過去已發生過的事，用過去式。「現在來台灣定居」，表示常態的事件，用現在式。「因此中文說得不是很好」，「thus」是副詞，「因此」的意思，也能當連接詞使用。**「英文不是說得很好」，「好」在此是副詞，修飾動詞「說」**，英文變化為：形容詞 good－副詞 well。

❶ 我從來沒看過老師如此生氣地說話：「你們坐好，閉嘴！」

I have never seen my teacher speak so furiously. "Sit up, and shut up!"

| 為什麼還能這樣翻 1 ··

　　「生氣」也可用「furious」表示，本句譯文需將形容詞加上「ly」變成副詞「furiously」，修飾受詞補語「speak」（因為動詞 see，可以有第二個動詞在其受詞後，為受詞補語，see 後面必須寫成原形動詞的形式）。語意已清楚明白在引號中的內容是老師說的話，故能在譯文中省略掉「she said」，不影響結構及語意。

❷ 先前住在美國，現在來台灣定居，因此中文說得不是很好。

She can't speak Chinese very well because they lived in America before.

| 為什麼還能這樣翻 2 ··

　　依照整篇文字內容的語意，若只譯出「她中文說得不是很好，因為先前住在美國」，也能清楚知道她是「現在來台灣定居」的結果，且不更改語意。助動詞「can」後面要用

原形動詞，因此「speak」在這裡不須加「s」。「because」
是連接詞，後面要有完整子句：主詞（they）＋過去式動詞
（lived）＋地方（in America）＋副詞（before）；子句中
的主詞若以「she」**取代**「they」表示亦可，但用「they」
將父母也涵括在內的方式，比較符合原來自我介紹時的敘
述，**也較有連貫性。**

全文翻譯

　　This semester, a new girl with red hair and a thin
figure has come to our class. When the teacher asked
her to introduce herself to us, there were still a few
classmates who kept on talking. I have never seen my
teacher talk so angrily, "Sit up, and shut up!" she said.
Everyone in the classroom became silent. Our new
classmate told us that her mother is Taiwanese, and her
father is American. They lived in America before, but
now they live in Taiwan, thus she can't speak Chinese
very well. Despite that, Taiwan isn't foreign to her.

關鍵技巧 **搞懂過去式的規則和不規則變化** ▶

關鍵例句搶先看 ◉

昨晚我待在醫院，陪伴剛動完清除脊椎骨刺手術的表姐。

I stayed in the hospital to accompany my cousin who had a spine spur removal operation last night.

基礎技巧提點

1 英文語法中，每個句子皆有其時態，其動詞／be ＋動詞，需配合時態有所變化。

2 動詞的過去式變化，分成規則和不規則。規則動詞過去式是在其字尾加「ed」；若字尾結尾是「e」，則只加「d」；若字尾結尾是子音加「y」，則刪除「y」再加上「ied」。如：end**ed**; fine**d**; accompan**ied**。

3 在不影響原意的情況下，需適時以英文的連接詞，使譯文更為通暢。

✏ 試著翻翻看▶ **試著翻畫底線的部分**

❶ <u>昨晚我待在醫院，陪伴剛動完清除脊椎骨刺手術的表姐。</u>表姐在凌晨三點醒來，我想應該是麻藥退去的原故；她說肚子餓，想吃點東西，❷ <u>可是她還沒辦法移動身體，必須維持平躺的姿勢，所以我只能給她一杯溫燕麥粥，讓她以吸管進食。</u>今天早上，醫生來病房的時候，他向表姐表示她仍得再住院三天，更囑咐需做三個月的復健療程，以幫助身體盡快恢復正常。

❶ _____

_____

_____

❷ _____

_____

_____

❶ 昨晚我待在醫院，陪伴剛動完清除脊椎骨刺手術的表姐。

I stayed in the hospital to accompany my cousin who had a spine spur removal operation last night.

| 為什麼這樣翻 1 ⋯⋯⋯⋯⋯⋯⋯⋯⋯⋯⋯⋯⋯⋯⋯⋯⋯⋯⋯⋯

　　「昨晚我待在醫院」，可判定是過去式文法，接續敘述的內容，亦需以過去式表示。「待；留」，**動詞「stay」**的過去式是規則形式，直接加「ed」。

　　「陪伴剛動完清除脊椎骨刺手術的表姐」這句，以關係代名詞「who」，代表在它之前的名詞「my cousin」，**進而**補充形容是「剛動完清除脊椎骨刺手術」。接受某種手術，英文以動詞「have」表示，為不規則的過去式動詞，「have-had」。

❷ 可是她還沒辦法移動身體，必須維持平躺的姿勢，所以我只能給她一杯溫燕麥粥，讓她以吸管進食。

But she wasn't able to move her body and had to stay in a lying position, so all I could do was give her a cup of warm oatmeal and let her take it with a straw.

| 為什麼這樣翻 2 ···

　　為前文的接續敘述，是過去式文法。「可是她還沒辦法移動身體」，過去式的 be 動詞配合名詞主詞為第三人稱單數「she」，因此用「was」。「必須」是「have to」，過去式為「had to」。助動詞「能－can」的過去式是「could」。「讓她以吸管進食」，動詞「讓－let」過去式為不規則形式，「let－let」。在動詞「let」其受詞（her）後的第二個動詞（take）是受詞補語，let 後方的受詞補語要寫成原形動詞的形式。

❶ 昨晚我待在醫院，陪伴剛動完清除脊椎骨刺手術的表姐。

I stayed in the hospital with my cousin last night after she had a spine spur removal operation.

| 為什麼還能這樣翻 1 ⋯⋯⋯⋯⋯⋯⋯⋯⋯⋯⋯⋯⋯⋯⋯⋯⋯⋯

　　此句指過去發生的事，須使用過去式文法，並將動詞改為過去式動詞「stayed」和「had」。可以用從屬子句連接詞（after）連接 主要子句 （I stayed in the hospital with my cousin last night）和從屬子句（she had a spine spur removal operation）。

❷ 可是她還沒辦法移動身體，必須維持在平躺的姿勢，所以我只能給她一杯溫燕麥粥，讓她以吸管進食。

As she was unable to move her body and had to remain in a lying position, all I could do was help her take a cup of warm oatmeal through a straw.

| 為什麼還能這樣翻 2 ⋯⋯⋯⋯⋯⋯⋯⋯⋯⋯⋯⋯⋯⋯⋯⋯⋯⋯

　　「沒辦法」，也就是「不能」的意思，可用過去式助動詞「couldn't＝過去式 be 動詞（was）unable to」表示。

「以吸管進食」，寫成受詞（her）【在這裡的 her 為 help 的受詞】＋受詞補語的及物動詞（take）＋名詞片語（a cup of warm oatmeal）＋介系詞（through）＋名詞（a straw）」。

全文翻譯

I stayed in the hospital to accompany my cousin who had a spine spur removal operation last night. She woke up at 3am; I supposed the anesthetic had faded. She said she felt hungry, and would like to eat something. But she wasn't able to move her body and had to stay in a lying position, so all I could do was give her a cup of warm oatmeal and let her take it with a straw. When the doctor came to the ward this morning, he told my cousin that she has to stay in hospital for another three days. He also advised a three month session of rehabilitation to help my cousin get back to normal as quickly as possible.

3-5 「再過一、兩年」的英文怎麼翻？時態上要注意什麼？

關鍵技巧 學會「未來完成式」！ ▶

關鍵例句搶先看 ◉

我期許自己再過一、兩年，能夠學會合作勝於爭吵的道理。

I expect that in one or two years' time, I will have learnt that it is better to cooperate than to fight.

基礎技巧提點

1 未來完成式，用於描述未來的某個時候，已經完成的動作。

2 未來完成式的結構是：will have ＋動詞的過去分詞。

3 英文語法需符合正確文法時態。

4 譯文需符合英文語法與恰當的標點符號，不需配合中文標點符號。

5 表示年齡的數值，可以阿拉伯數字或英文字譯出皆可，唯需擇一，以達文章整體的一致性。

✎ **試著翻翻看▶** **試著翻畫底線的部分**

　　我很愛我的哥哥。我現在七歲，哥哥比我大兩歲。他很照顧我，也很愛我，可是每當我們兩個都想要做同一件事情時，就會互不相讓，也因此常常鬧得不開心收場。❶ 哥哥總是跟我說，等我跟他一樣大的時候，就會克服這個問題且能獨當一面，不需要別人的協助。可是我相信自己就能做得到，所以跟他爭論，也不讓他幫忙。我不得不承認，哥哥是對的。很多事，我沒有辦法自己完成。如果有哥哥的協助，事情的確會順利很多。❷ 我期許自己再過一、兩年，能夠學會合作勝於爭吵的道理。

❶ _____

_____

_____

❷ _____

_____

_____

❶ 哥哥總是跟我說，等我跟他一樣大的時候，就會克服這個問題且能獨當一面，不需要別人的協助。

My brother always tells me that when I am his age, I will have overcome this problem and be capable of doing everything on my own without anyone's assistance.

| 為什麼這樣翻 1 ·······································

　　「哥哥總是跟我說，等我跟他一樣大的時候」，為現在式文法，時間點為「等我跟他一樣大的時候」，是指未來的某天；而「就會克服這個問題且能獨當一面，不需要別人的協助」，表示未來某時會已經完成的動作，故用「未來完成式」：will have ＋動詞的過去分詞，也就是括弧中動詞三態裡，最後面的那個（overcome-overcame-overcome）。

❷ 我期許自己再過一、兩年，能夠學會合作勝於爭吵的道理。

I expect that in one or two years' time, I will have learnt that it is better to cooperate than to fight.

| 為什麼這樣翻 2 ⋯⋯⋯⋯⋯⋯⋯⋯⋯⋯⋯⋯⋯⋯⋯⋯⋯⋯⋯⋯

　　「一、兩年」，亦可以阿拉伯數字（1、2）表示，唯需有一致性，不以數字與英文字混用表示。

　　「能夠學會合作勝於爭吵的道理」，其時間點為「再過一、兩年」，是指未來的一、兩年之後，就能夠學會某事，故用未來完成式：will have＋動詞的過去分詞，也就是括弧中動詞三態裡，最後面的那個；learnt 和 learned 是通用的（learn-learnt (learned) -learnt (learned)）。

❶ 哥哥總是跟我說，等我跟他一樣大的時候，就會克服這個問題且能獨當一面，不需要別人的協助。

My brother has always told me that when I am as old as he is now, I will no longer have this problem, but will be able to do everything myself without assistance.

| 為什麼還能這樣翻 1 ··

　　「哥哥總是跟我說」，亦可用現在完成式：has＋動詞的過去分詞（tell-told-told）表示。「就會克服這個問題且能獨當一面，不需要別人的協助」，亦可使用未來式表示：主要子句（未來式）＋英文逗號（,）＋並列連接詞（but）＋主要子句（未來式）。「can」的未來式必須寫作「will be able to」。

❷ 我期許自己再過一、兩年，能夠學會合作勝於爭吵的道理。

I hope that in a couple of years' time, I will have learnt that cooperation is better than fighting.

| 為什麼還能這樣翻 2 ··

　　「再過一、兩年」，亦可以「in a couple of years'

time」的時間副詞表示，表示「一、兩年後」。「合作勝於爭吵」亦寫作：不可數名詞（cooperation）＋be 動詞（is）＋比較級（better than）＋動名詞（fighting）；動名詞是名詞。

I love my brother very much. I am seven now, and my brother is two years older than me. My brother loves me very much and takes good care of me, but when it comes to both of wanting to do the same thing, we do not make concessions to each other; therefore, it normally ends up unhappily. My brother always tells me that when I am his age, I will have overcome this problem and be capable of doing everything on my own without anyone's assistance. But I believe that I can do it just fine, so I argue with him and refuse his help. I hate to admit that my brother is right. There are many things I can't do alone. It would be easier if I had my brother's help. I expect that in one or two years' time, I will have learnt that it is better to cooperate than to fight.

中文的「有……」，在英文一定是「There is / are」嗎？

關鍵技巧 不一定，你還有其他的翻法！ ▶

關鍵例句搶先看 ⊙

上週三，社區附近新開了一家叫「隨便」（Whatever）的咖啡廳。

Last Wednesday, there was a newly opened café in my neighborhood which is named "Whatever".

基礎技巧提點

1 看完整段、整句後再下筆。

2 從中文語意辨讀每個句子的各別時態。

3 了解中文語意後，再譯成英文，譯意不譯字。

4 中文標點符號，圓括號「（）」用於標註插入語或修飾評論。

5 本身為英文名的名詞，直接譯回原文，不需再附上中文譯文。

✏️ **試著翻翻看▶** **試著翻畫底線的部分**

❶ 上週三，社區附近新開了一家叫「隨便」（Whatever）的咖啡廳。廣告上寫著滿三百元即可免費外送。開幕第一週，全面八五折。

今天下午約了幾位朋友來家裡，於是我打電話請咖啡廳外送。點了三杯中杯熱拿鐵、三塊蛋糕：黑森林（black forest）、起司蛋糕（cheese cake）和提拉米蘇（tiramisu），折扣後為台幣三百三十二元。❷ 外送人員在二十分鐘內將咖啡及蛋糕送達。咖啡和蛋糕美味極了。我們度過了一個愉快的下午茶時光。

❶ _____

_____

_____

❷ _____

_____

_____

❶ 上週三,社區附近新開了一家叫「隨便」(Whatever)的咖啡廳。

Last Wednesday, there was a newly opened café in my neighborhood which is named "Whatever".

| 為什麼這樣翻 1 ⋯⋯⋯⋯⋯⋯⋯⋯⋯⋯⋯⋯⋯⋯⋯⋯⋯⋯⋯⋯⋯⋯⋯⋯⋯⋯⋯⋯

　　英文文法中,用來表示一個地方有什麼東西,本句是以過去式時態「there was / there were」表示,there **為假主詞,後面的名詞不可加冠詞(the)或所有格**(my, your, his, our, Matt's⋯)。時間副詞可放在主詞前。

　　「新開幕」為「newly opened」,台灣常見以直接譯單字的方式誤譯為「new open」。英文引號用於指明:單字有不尋常含意的狀態,在這做為店名。

❷ 外送人員在二十分鐘內將咖啡及蛋糕送達。咖啡和蛋糕美味極了。

The delivery guy delivered my order within twenty minutes. Both their coffee and cake tasted delicious.

| 為什麼這樣翻 2 ·······

「二十分鐘內」，是不到二十分鐘的意思，以介系詞「within」表示不超出（某段時間）；在（某段時間）之內。**「咖啡和蛋糕」泛指大家享用過的咖啡和蛋糕，單字本身能以不可數表示。**當主詞為兩種事物（複數）時，以「both」表示「兩者都是」的狀態。兩句皆為過去式文法。

❶ 上週三，社區附近新開了一家叫「隨便」（Whatever）的
咖啡廳。

Last Wednesday, a new café called "Whatever"
opened in my neighborhood.

| 為什麼還能這樣翻 1 ....

　　「社區附近」是指敘述者的社區附近，譯作「in my
neighborhood」。「新開」也可譯作「新的咖啡廳」，即
為「a new café」。皆為過去式文法。

❷ 外送人員在二十分鐘內將咖啡及蛋糕送達。咖啡和蛋糕美味
極了。

In less than twenty minutes, the delivery guy brought
us our order. Coffee and cake were both delicious.

| 為什麼還能這樣翻 2 ....

　　「二十分鐘內」，亦可以「少於二十分鐘」的說法譯
出，**時間副詞可放在主詞之前**。「咖啡及蛋糕送達」，依照
前文可清楚知道，這是點購的餐點，因此可以「our order」
表示即可，且需使用過去式，因為敘述這件事情時，東西已

經送達。「咖啡和蛋糕美味極了」，是過去式，表示當時的評語。「both」表示兩者都是，可當形容詞和代名詞。

全文翻譯

Last Wednesday, there was a newly opened café in my neighborhood which is named "Whatever". On the advertisement, it says "Order more than NT.300 and you can have free delivery. During the first week of opening, everything has 15% off."

I have invited some friends to come to my house this afternoon, so I telephoned the café and asked them to deliver. I ordered three medium Latté and three slices of cake-black forest, cheese cake and tiramisu. The delivery guy delivered my order within twenty minutes. Both their coffee and cake tasted delicious. My friends and I enjoyed our afternoon tea time very much.

中文的「太……而不能……」句型，英文也有同樣的說法嗎？

關鍵技巧 中英文法概念也有相通的地方！ ▶

關鍵例句搶先看 ▶

他認為我的身高太矮，不適合打籃球。

He thinks I am too short to play basketball.

基礎技巧提點

1 從事球類運動，英文是以片語：「play＋球類」表示，其「play」是及物動詞，後面要有受詞。

2 「和朋友玩」的「玩」，是不及物動詞，沒有受詞，譯作「play（不及物動詞）with（介系詞）my friends（名詞）」

3 從中文語意中，辨別出英文語法中的時態。

4 看完整個句子、段落後，再下筆。

5 在不影響原意的情況下，適時加入英文的連接詞，使譯文符合語法且通暢。

✏️ **試著翻翻看▶** **試著翻畫底線的部分**

　　長大後，我想當籃球員。從八歲開始，只要電視有轉播 NBA 球賽，我一定每場收看。❶ 學校的籃球社團教練不讓我加入籃球社團，因為他認為我的身高太矮，不適合打籃球。儘管如此，我並沒有放棄，除了調整飲食之外，也會在空閒時間跟朋友一起打籃球。❷ 現在我已經跟我一百六十公分的母親一樣高。希望到了明年，我能長高到一百七十五公分，並加入籃球社團。

❶ _____

_____

_____

❷ _____

_____

_____

❶ 學校的籃球社團教練不讓我加入籃球社團，因為他認為我的身高太矮，不適合打籃球。

..., but the coach of my school's basketball team wouldn't let me join the team because he thinks I am too short to play basketball.

| 為什麼這樣翻 1 ⋯⋯⋯⋯⋯⋯⋯⋯⋯⋯⋯⋯⋯⋯⋯⋯⋯⋯⋯⋯⋯⋯⋯

　　「籃球社團教練不讓我加入籃球社團」，是過去式文法。「因為他認為我的身高太矮，不適合打籃球」，是現在式文法。「太⋯⋯做某件事」或「太⋯⋯以致於」，與形容詞連用，在英文文法中是以「too＋形容詞＋to＋某件事」表示。

❷ 現在我已經跟我一百六十公分的母親一樣高。

Now, I am as tall as my mother whose height is 160 centimeters.

| 為什麼這樣翻 2 ·································

　　副詞（now）可放在主詞前面，但需在副詞後加逗號。「跟……一樣；像……一樣」，在英文文法中以「as... as」表示，用於表達兩者相比較後，相等的狀態，與形容詞或副詞連用，**可用於肯定或否定的語意中**。譯作「as tall（形容詞）as my mother」。關係代名詞「whose」帶領的形容詞子句，用來表示它之前的「人或動物**的**」。

❶ 學校的籃球社團教練不讓我加入籃球社團，因為他認為我的身高太矮，不適合打籃球。

..., but the coach of my school's basketball team wouldn't let me join the team because he thinks I am not tall enough to play basketball.

| 為什麼還能這樣翻 1 ⋯⋯⋯⋯⋯⋯⋯⋯⋯⋯⋯⋯⋯⋯⋯⋯⋯

「我的身高太矮，不適合打籃球」，意即「不夠高打籃球」的意思。亦可譯作「not＋形容詞＋enough to＋做某件事」，即「not tall enough to play basketball」。

❷ 現在我已經跟我一百六十公分的母親一樣高。

My mother is 160 cm tall, and I am as tall as her now.

| 為什麼還能這樣翻 2 ⋯⋯⋯⋯⋯⋯⋯⋯⋯⋯⋯⋯⋯⋯⋯⋯⋯

主要子句以「我的母親一百六十公分高：My mother is 160 cm tall」表示，加上並列子句連接詞「, and」，再加上主要子句「我現在跟她一樣高：I am as tall as her now」。辨識度高的身高單位僅能以英文縮寫表示。

When I grow up, I want to be a basketball player. I have never missed an NBA match on TV since I was eight, but the coach of my school's basketball team wouldn't let me join the team because he thinks I am too short to play basketball. However, I didn't give up. I not only adjusted my diet habits but also play basketball with my friends in my free time. Now, I am as tall as my mother whose height is 160 centimeters. Hopefully by next year, I can grow to 175 centimeters and then join the basketball team.

英文中使用「進行式」的時機是何時？過去也有進行式嗎？

關鍵技巧 好好用中文理解英文文法，英文文法、翻譯進步更快！ ▶

關鍵例句搶先看 ◉

我原本計劃今天晚上帶女朋友去看場電影，現在看來，是沒辦法去了。

I was planning to take my girlfriend out for a movie tonight, but now, it doesn't seem possible to go to the movies.

基礎技巧提點

1 英文語法中，已揭露該句或該段落的名詞主詞後，在接續的敘述中，多以代名詞／指示代名詞／其他名詞表示其主詞

2 已是英文名的專有名詞，直接譯回原文，不需再附上中文譯文。

3 依中文語意譯出英文時，**需符合英文語法中的時態與詞性變化**。

✎ 試著翻翻看▶ **試著翻畫底線的部分**

　　昨天晚上雨勢猛烈，不過我今天早上起床時，陽光普照。
❶ 吃完早餐後，在我出門上班的途中，風勢十分強勁，幾乎要
把我整個人吹走。下午三點，當我步行到公車站準備搭車回家
時，目擊了一場車禍，幸好只是小擦撞，無人受傷。

　　回到家後，我接到同事的電話，說晚上六點要去梅爾酒吧
（Mayer's Pub）替同事舉行慶生派對。❷ 我原本計劃今天晚
上帶女朋友去看場電影，現在看來，是沒辦法去了。

❶ _____

_____

_____

❷ _____

_____

_____

❶ 吃完早餐後，在我出門上班的途中，風勢十分強勁，幾乎要把我整個人吹走。

After breakfast, on my way to work, the wind was blowing hard and it nearly blew me away.

| 為什麼這樣翻 1 ....

「風勢十分強勁」，依照前文語意，可以知道是表達過去某個動作發生時，正在進行的動作，因此需使用過去進行式文法，該文法的句型結構為：**主詞（the wind）＋過去式be 動詞（was）＋動詞的現在分詞（blowing）＋副詞（hard）**。

副詞（hard）修飾動詞的現在分詞，表示「風吹得強勁地」；亦可用於形容雨勢的猛烈程度：rain hard。hard 為規則的形容詞／副詞－hard－hard。

❷ 我原本計劃今天晚上帶女朋友去看場電影，現在看來，是沒辦法去了。

I was planning to take my girlfriend out for a movie tonight, but now, it doesn't seem possible to go to the movies.

| 為什麼這樣翻 2 ···

　　「我原本計劃今天晚上帶女朋友去看場電影」，表示過去正要進行的事，因此是用過去進行式文法。該文法的句型結構為：**主詞（I）＋過去式 be 動詞（was）＋動詞的現在分詞（planning）＋不定詞（to take）＋直接受詞（my girlfriend）＋副詞（out）＋介系詞（for）＋間接受詞（a movie）＋時間副詞（tonight）**。

❶ 吃完早餐後，在我出門上班的途中，風勢十分強勁，幾乎要把我整個人吹走。

A strong wind was blowing when I was on my way to work after breakfast, and it nearly blew me away.

| 為什麼還能這樣翻 1 ⋯⋯⋯⋯⋯⋯⋯⋯⋯⋯⋯⋯⋯⋯⋯⋯⋯⋯⋯⋯⋯⋯

　　表達過去某個動作發生時，正在進行的動作，因此需使用過去進行式文法。本句亦可解讀作：「當我吃完早餐出門上班的途中，風勢十分強勁」，並先翻「風勢（吹得）十分強勁」。**其中用來形容風勢的形容詞，可以「strong」表示，形容詞（strong）修飾名詞（the wind），但不可用來形容雨勢。**

❷ 我原本計劃今天晚上帶女朋友去看場電影，現在看來，是沒辦法去了。

I was planning to take my girlfriend out to see a movie tonight, but it doesn't seem possible to go now.

| 為什麼還能這樣翻 2 ⋯⋯⋯⋯⋯⋯⋯⋯⋯⋯⋯⋯⋯⋯⋯

「我原本計劃今天晚上帶女朋友去看場電影」，表示過去正要進行的事，因此是用過去進行式文法。以並列子句連接詞（, but）連接兩個主要子句，第二個主要子句為現在式文法，其代名詞主詞「it」，代表第一個主要子句敘述的事情。看電影除了可用「out for a movie」、「go to the movies」表達外，也可以翻成「see a movie」。

全文翻譯

It rained hard last night although the sun was shining brightly when I got up this morning. After breakfast, on my way to work, the wind was blowing hard and it nearly blew me away. At three o'clock in the afternoon when I was walking to the bus station to take a bus home, I witnessed a car accident. Fortunately, it was just two cars that had a minor bump into each other and it caused no injuries.

After I got home, I got a call from my colleague, saying that there is going to be a birthday party at Mayer's Pub for one of our colleagues. I was planning to take my girlfriend out for a movie tonight, but now, it doesn't seem possible to go to the movies.

什麼是「反身代名詞」?

關鍵技巧 **學會反身代名詞,提升中翻英的修辭技巧** ▶

關鍵例句搶先看 ◉

前幾天,我跟爸爸說我想學煮飯,可是爸爸說:「你會燙到,不行!」

A few days ago, I told my dad I wanted to learn how to cook, but my dad said, "No! You will burn yourself."

基礎技巧提點

1 需看完整個句子、段落,辨別每個句子所屬的時態。譯意不譯字。

2 反身代名詞所指的對象是該句的主詞,意即受詞和主詞所指的是同一人。

3 反身代名詞和「by」連用,意指獨立完成某事。

4 英文中的引號「" "」,用於引述人物話語,或是強調內容。

✏️ **試著翻翻看▶** **試著翻畫底線的部分**

　　為什麼大人都不信任小孩的做事能力？❶ <u>喜歡命令我們：「去做這個」、「不可以這樣做」、「這樣做才對」、「你自己處理」</u>，高標準地要求我們獨力，但卻又不放手讓我們用自己的方式去做。

　　❷ <u>前幾天，我跟爸爸說我想學煮飯，可是爸爸說：「你會燙到，不行！」</u>。媽媽要我去洗盤子，卻又一直站在我身旁「指導」我該怎麼洗才對；我直接把洗碗精擠在菜瓜布上，她馬上制止我，說這樣不對；我已經用水把盤子沖乾淨了，但是她就硬是要再沖一次水，因為她覺得我一定沒沖乾淨。

❶ _____

_____

_____

❷ _____

_____

_____

❶ 喜歡命令我們：「去做這個」、「不可以這樣做」、「這樣做才對」、「你自己處理」。

They like to command us: "Go and do this." "You can't do that." "You have to do it like this." "Go and deal with it yourself."

| 為什麼這樣翻 1 ··

　　每個引號中的句子皆為完整句子，故需有句號「.」才符合英文語法。「你自己處理」，祈使句其主詞是「you」，但是省略；反身代名詞所指的**即是「你自己處理」**這句的主詞「you」，所以用「yourself」。

❷ 前幾天，我跟爸爸說我想學煮飯，可是爸爸說：「你會燙到，不行！」

A few days ago, I told my dad I wanted to learn how to cook, but my dad said, "No! You will burn yourself."

| 為什麼這樣翻 2 ⋯⋯⋯⋯⋯⋯⋯⋯⋯⋯⋯⋯⋯⋯⋯⋯⋯

　　時間點為「前幾天」，為過去式文法。

　　時間副詞「a few days ago」，也可以寫在主詞之前，再加上英文逗號（,）。本句結構為：時間副詞（a few days ago）＋英文逗號（,）＋主要子句（I told my dad I wanted to learn how to cook）＋逗號（,）＋並列連接詞（but）＋主要子句（my dad said, "No! You will burn yourself."）。**中文雖然沒有將燙到「誰」寫出來，但從語意可理解為「燙到自己」，英文翻為「yourself」**。

🖋 也可以這麼翻

❶ 喜歡命令我們：「去做這個」、「不可以這樣做」、「這樣做才對」、「你自己處理」。

They like to tell us what to do: "Go and do this." "You can't do that." "You have to do it like this." "Go and deal with it yourself."

| 為什麼還能這樣翻 1 ···

　　在英文中，用「tell」來表達要某個人做某件事，即有「支配；強制；命令；規定」的意思。

❷ 前幾天，我跟爸爸說我想學煮飯，可是爸爸說：「你會燙到，不行！」

I asked my dad if I could learn how to cook a few days ago, but my dad replied, "No, You will burn yourself!"

| 為什麼還能這樣翻 2 ···

　　這句的時間副詞寫在句子的最後。「我跟爸爸說我想學煮飯，可是爸爸說」，意即「我問爸爸……，可是我爸給我的答案是……」，皆為過去式文法。「你會燙到」，是預設的立場，還沒發生，所以使用未來式文法。

Why don't adults trust children's ability to do things? They like to command us: "Go and do this." "You can't do that." "You have to do it like this." "Go and deal with it yourself." They ask for a high standard of independence, but they wouldn't allow us to do anything in our own way.

A few days ago, I told my dad I wanted to learn how to cook, but my dad said, "No! You will burn yourself." My mom asked me to wash the dishes, but she kept standing beside me and "instructed" me how to wash them. I put the washing up liquid directly on the sponge; then she told me off immediately. After I rinsed the dishes, she insisted on rinsing them again because she thought I could not have rinsed them properly.

中翻英時如何避免「中式英文」？

關鍵技巧 用「外國人的思維」，學他們慣有的語法：「應該（supposed to）」、「以前都是（used to）」！ ▶

關鍵例句搶先看 ▶

當我還在就讀國小和國中時，都是自己走路上學。

When I was in elementary school and junior high school, I used to walk to school.

基礎技巧提點

1 「應該」是「supposed to＋原形動詞」，用於表示預期或期望，是 be 動詞文法，其 be 動詞文法有現在式和過去式。

2 「以前都是」是「used to＋原形動詞」，用於描述習慣性的動作，亦或是以前發生過，但現在已不再發生的行為。

3 若表示長度的單位有特定縮寫形式或符號，且十分常見，譯文可不譯出英文字。

✎ 試著翻翻看▶ 試著翻畫底線的部分

❶ 當我還在就讀國小和國中時，都是自己走路上學。可是我現在就讀的高中，離我家約十五公里的距離，所以每天早上，我得在六點十五鐘出門，走路到公車站，然後搭乘六點三十分的公車去學校。

❷ 我應該在早上七點鐘到校，可是今天我上學遲到了，不是因為我睡過頭，而是公車沒有來。我在公車站等了近半個小時，仍不見公車蹤影，最後才放棄繼續枯等，改搭計程車去上學。公車通常都很準時進站，希望今天早上的情形，以後不會再發生。

❶ _____

_____

_____

❷ _____

_____

_____

❶ 當我還在就讀國小和國中時，都是自己走路上學。

When I was in elementary school and junior high school, I used to walk to school.

| 為什麼這樣翻 1 ⋯⋯⋯⋯⋯⋯⋯⋯⋯⋯⋯⋯⋯⋯⋯⋯⋯⋯⋯⋯⋯⋯⋯⋯⋯

　　從「當我還在就讀國小和國中時」，可判定為過去式文法。敘述當時「都是自己走路上學」，即表示現在不再自己走路上學。**用「used to」來描述以前發生但現在不再發生的行為，該句句型結構為：主詞＋used（過去式動詞）＋to 原形動詞。**

❷ 我應該在早上七點鐘到校，可是今天我上學遲到了，不是因為我睡過頭，而是公車沒有來。

I was supposed to be at school at 7 o'clock this morning, but I wasn't, and the reason why I was late was not because I overslept but that the bus didn't show up.

| 為什麼這樣翻 2 ·······································

　　「我應該在早上七點鐘到校，可是今天我上學遲到了」，語意顯示出預期與期望的意涵，是**過去式** be **動詞**文法，結構為：**主詞＋過去式** be **動詞＋**supposed（**形容詞**）**＋**to **原形動詞**。本段接續的敘述，皆為過去式文法。

❶ 當我還在就讀國小和國中時，都是自己走路上學。

I usually walked to school when I was an elementary school and junior high school student.

| 為什麼還能這樣翻 1 ⋯⋯⋯⋯⋯⋯⋯⋯⋯⋯⋯⋯⋯⋯⋯

　　「當我還在就讀國小和國中時」，即「當我還是國小和國中生時」，皆為過去式 be 動詞文法。以前的那時候「都是自己走路上學」，亦可直接以過去式動詞文法表示。過去式動詞「walk」是規則形式，在字尾加「ed」。

❷ 我應該在早上七點鐘到校，可是今天我上學遲到了，不是因為我睡過頭，而是公車沒有來。

I should have been at school at 7 o'clock this morning, but I wasn't. I got up on time, but the bus never showed up.

| 為什麼還能這樣翻 2 ⋯⋯⋯⋯⋯⋯⋯⋯⋯⋯⋯⋯⋯⋯⋯

　　「不是因為我睡過頭」，即「我準時起床」的意思；「準時」－「on time」。此句為過去式動詞文法，過去式

動詞「起床」（get up) 的 get 是不規則動詞，原形和過去式為「get-got」。「公車沒有來」，即「沒有出現」，其過去式動詞「show」是規則形式，在字尾加「ed」。

全文翻譯

When I was in elementary school and junior high school, I used to walk to school. Since the high school I am in now is about fifteen kilometers from where I live, I have to leave home at quarter past six every morning to walk to the bus station, and then take the six-thirty bus to school.

I was supposed to be at school at 7 o'clock this morning, but I wasn't, and the reason why I was late was not because I overslept but that the bus didn't show up. I waited at the bus station for half an hour, but there was still no sign of it. In the end, I gave up waiting and took a taxi to school instead. The bus usually approaches to the station on time, and I certainly hope what happened this morning won't happen again.

翻譯英文句 如何更簡潔？

關鍵技巧 學會「分詞構句」！ ▶

關鍵例句搶先看 ▶

歷經一連串的食安風暴，難免讓人想減少外食的次數，盡量自己下廚。

Having been through a cluster of food security problems, it is inevitable that people want to reduce the frequency of eating out and try to cook at home as much as possible.

基礎技巧提點

1 從中文語意辨讀每個句子的各別時態。

2 中文標點符號與英文標點符號的使用方法與時機不同，不依中文句中的標點符號譯作英文。

3 了解中文語意後，再譯成英文，不逐字譯，應在不影響原意的情況下，以符合英文語法的方式譯出。

✏️ 試著翻翻看 ▶ 試著翻畫底線的部分

吃什麼才安心？❶ <u>歷經一連串的食安風暴，難免讓人想減少外食的次數，盡量自己下廚。</u>可是，自己煮的就一定沒問題嗎？答案是否定的。食材的品質與來源，以及烹調方式，是食物是否能安全食用的關鍵。

要擁有健康，除了吃得好，也要配合運動。❷ <u>我和家人每週運動三次以上，每次維持四十到六十分鐘。下個月還準備挑戰攻頂玉山（Mt. Jade）。</u>

❶ _____

_____

_____

❷ _____

_____

_____

❶ 歷經一連串的食安風暴，難免讓人想減少外食的次數，盡量自己下廚。

Having been through a cluster of food security problems, it is inevitable that people want to reduce the frequency of eating out and try to cook at home as much as possible.

| 為什麼這樣翻 1 ··

「歷經一連串的食安風暴」為現在完成式分詞構句，從中文語意中辨別出為已經發生的敘述。

「難免讓人想減少外食的次數，盡量自己下廚」為現在式文法。**現在完成式分詞構句結構為：having＋過去分詞。**此句是以「現在分詞開始的片語」為開頭＋主要子句，兩者可前後互換。適時加入連接詞，以接續述敘的方式讓所要表達的句子一氣呵成，便能達到讓句子簡潔明快的目的。

❷ 我和家人每週運動三次以上，每次維持四十到六十分鐘。下個月還準備挑戰攻頂玉山（Mt. Jade）。

We exercise three times a week; each time for around 40 to 60 minutes. We are going to climb Mt. Jade next month and step onto its peak.

| 為什麼這樣翻 2 ⋯⋯⋯⋯⋯⋯⋯⋯⋯⋯⋯⋯⋯⋯⋯⋯⋯⋯⋯⋯⋯

「我和家人每週運動三次以上，每次維持四十到六十分鐘。」為現在式文法，注意代名詞主詞的用法。「下個月還準備挑戰攻頂玉山（Mt. Jade）。」是未來式文法，代名詞主詞用「we」表示「我和家人」。未來式動詞文法助動詞「will」＋原形動詞＝「be 動詞＋going to」＋原形動詞。

❶ 歷經一連串的食安風暴，難免讓人想減少外食的次數，盡量自己下廚。

As a result of having been through a series of food safety problems, people want to try not to eat out so often and cook at home as much as possible.

| 為什麼還能這樣翻 1 ⋯⋯⋯⋯⋯⋯⋯⋯⋯⋯⋯⋯⋯⋯⋯⋯⋯⋯⋯

亦可譯作「歷經一連串的食安風暴，結果導致大家試圖不那麼常外食，並盡量自己下廚」。「as a result」可當片語寫在句首，亦可作為副詞連接詞，本句亦可譯為「Having been through a series of food safety problems; as a result, people want to try not to eat out so often and cook at home as much as possible.」，也就是將連接詞接在兩句中間，另外需要注意的，後面的主詞（people）需要和分詞構句相符，也就是必須要是「人」來歷經一連串的食安風暴，不能是「人」以外的主詞。

❷ 我和家人每週運動三次以上，每次維持四十到六十分鐘。下個月還準備挑戰攻頂玉山（Mt. Jade）。

My family and I do around forty to sixty minutes of

exercise three times a week. We will hike up Mt. Jade next month as a challenge for us.

| 為什麼還能這樣翻 2

「I；我」是用在其他代名詞主詞之後，譯作「My family and I」；「下個月還準備挑戰攻頂玉山」亦可譯作「下個月挑戰攻頂玉山，**當作我們的挑戰**」。

What is safe to eat? Having been through a cluster of food security problems, it is inevitable that people want to reduce the frequency of eating out and try to cook at home as much as possible. Is the food that you cook at home totally safe to eat? The answer is "NO". Ingredients, quality, source and the way you cook are the crucial elements to determine if the food is safe or not.

To be healthy, you should not only eat well but also do exercise regularly. We exercise three times a week; each time for around 40 to 60 minutes. We are going to climb Mt. Jade next month and step onto its peak.

5-2 常有人說你的英文句子太長嗎？

那更要學會使用「代名詞：anywhere、everywhere、someone、some things」！ ▸

關鍵例句搶先看 ▶

我很喜歡觀察牠們，我覺得牠們有些事情跟人類相似。

I like to observe them very much because I think some things about them are very similar to humans.

基礎技巧提點

1. 先看完整句、整段，依文意判定英文語法的時態。

2. 任何地方－「anywhere」，用於否定句中。每個地方－「everywhere」，用於肯定句中。

3. 某人－「someone／somebody」，用於肯定句中；不要跟一些人－「some people」搞混。

4. 一些事－「some things」，用於肯定句中；不要跟某件事／某個東西－「something」搞混。

📝 **試著翻翻看▶** **試著翻畫底線的部分**

　　我養了兩隻烏龜－李歐（Leo）和拉斐爾（Raphael）。我每天餵牠們吃二次飼料和蝦乾，每天讓牠們在陽台曬太陽半小時。❶ 我很喜歡觀察牠們，我覺得牠們有些事情跟人類相似。牠們會爬上我替他們準備的岩石上睡覺或休息，彷彿岩石是牠們的床。

　　可是昨天晚上，當我要餵牠們吃飼料時，我卻發現李歐不見了！❷ 我遍尋房間的每個角落，仍到處都找不到牠，於是我問了宿舍裡的每個人，但是沒有人看到我養的烏龜。總之，我確信李歐一定是被人帶走了。

❶ _____

_____

_____

❷ _____

_____

_____

❶ 我很喜歡觀察牠們，我覺得牠們有些事情跟人類相似。

I like to observe them very much because I think some things about them are very similar to humans.

| 為什麼這樣翻 1 ⋯⋯⋯⋯⋯⋯⋯⋯⋯⋯⋯⋯⋯⋯⋯⋯⋯⋯⋯⋯⋯

　　加上連接詞「because」，連接兩個子句，使語意更完整、通暢。兩個子句的時態皆為現在式。相似－「similar (to)」＋名詞。一些事－「some things」；「一些」是形容詞（some），修飾複數形或不可數名詞，「事」是可數名詞（thing），需寫成複數形式。

❷ 我遍尋房間的每個角落，仍到處都找不到牠，於是我問了宿舍裡的每個人，但是沒有人看到我養的烏龜。

I searched everywhere in my room, but I couldn't find it anywhere, so I asked everyone in the dorm, but no one had seen it.

| 為什麼這樣翻 2 ⋯⋯⋯⋯⋯⋯⋯⋯⋯⋯⋯⋯⋯⋯⋯⋯⋯

　　中文的「到處；每個地方」，在英文的肯定句中用「everywhere」；在否定句中用「anywhere」。中文的「每個人」，在英文的肯定句中用「everyone/everybody」；否定句中用「anyone/anybody」。

　　中文的「沒有人／沒有任何地方／沒有任何事」，在英文語法中以肯定句形式表示，但實質語意為否定的意思，用「no one; no body/ nowhere/ nothing」。

🖋 也可以這麼翻

❶ 我很喜歡觀察牠們，我覺得牠們有些事情跟人類相似。

I like observing them very much because I think there are some things about them which are very similar to humans.

| 為什麼還能這樣翻 1 ·····································

　　動詞「喜歡」－「like」，後面用不定詞（to＋動詞）或動名詞（V＋ing），意思是一樣的。**「我覺得牠們有些事情跟人類相似」，亦可以關係代名詞（which）來帶領形容詞子句，代表在它之前的事／物（some things about them）。**

❷ 我遍尋房間的每個角落，仍到處都找不到牠，於是我問了宿舍裡的每個人，但是沒有人看到我養的烏龜。

I searched everywhere in my room, but there was no sign of it, then I asked everyone in the dorm, but no one had seen it.

| 為什麼還能這樣翻 2 ···

　　為了譯文的完整性與流暢度，需適時加上英文語法中的連接詞（but），以充分詮釋語意。「仍到處都找不到牠」，亦可譯作：主詞（there）＋過去式 be 動詞（was）＋形容詞（no）＋不可數名詞（sign）＋介系詞（of）＋代名詞受詞（it）。

全文翻譯

　　I have two pet turtles-Leo and Raphael. I feed them pellets and dried shrimps twice a day and let them stay in the sun for half an hour every day on the balcony. I like to observe them very much because I think some things about them are very similar to humans. They climb on the rock I prepared for them and sleep or rest there as if the rock is their bed.

　　But last night when I was going to feed them as usual, I found Leo missing! I searched everywhere in my room, but I couldn't find it anywhere, so I asked everyone in the dorm, but no one had seen it. Therefore, I am sure Leo must have been taken by someone.

5-3 either 和 neither 傻傻分不清嗎？

簡化英文句子，either 和 neither 其實很好用！ ▶

關鍵例句搶先看 ◉

我和朋友都不會游泳。

My friend doesn't know how to swim, and neither do I.

基礎技巧提點

1 在否定句中用 either 和 neither 表示－「也不」，避免字詞重複。

2 英文主詞在其隨後接續的敘述中，多以代名詞主詞／指示代名詞／其他名詞表示。

3 英文有時態、詞性變化，並適時加上連接詞，使譯文脈絡更為完整、通暢。

4 譯其意，不過度著墨於字詞的特定單字。

5 英文譯文需符合英文語法，不可以直譯的方式，逐字譯出。

✏️ **試著翻翻看 ▶** **試著翻畫底線的部分**

　　春節期間，我和朋友每天一起到運動中心運動。❶ <u>運動中心有游泳池，可是因為我和朋友都不會游泳</u>，就只打迴力球、網球，以及使用其他健身器材。我的朋友説，他有嘗試學游泳，但就是學不會，也因此消極地認為自己永遠都學不會游泳了。❷ <u>我安慰他説我也還不會游泳，並建議一同報名泳訓班。</u>在詢問了泳訓班的收費之後，我們決定報名，並立志要在暑假開始之前，學會游泳。

❶ ＿＿＿＿＿＿＿＿＿＿＿＿＿＿＿＿＿＿＿＿＿＿
＿＿＿＿＿＿＿＿＿＿＿＿＿＿＿＿＿＿＿＿＿＿＿＿
＿＿＿＿＿＿＿＿＿＿＿＿＿＿＿＿＿＿＿＿＿＿＿＿

❷ ＿＿＿＿＿＿＿＿＿＿＿＿＿＿＿＿＿＿＿＿＿＿
＿＿＿＿＿＿＿＿＿＿＿＿＿＿＿＿＿＿＿＿＿＿＿＿
＿＿＿＿＿＿＿＿＿＿＿＿＿＿＿＿＿＿＿＿＿＿＿＿

❶ 運動中心有游泳池，可是因為我和朋友都不會游泳

The sports center has a swimming pool, but as my friend doesn't know how to swim, and neither do I,...

| 為什麼這樣翻 1 ···

　　在否定句中，可用 neither 來避免字詞重複。用 neither 加一個動詞片語，將第二個子句改短。英文常見的寫法能將兩個連接詞寫在一起，連接接續的兩個子句。

　　本句為現在式（The sports center has a swimming pool）＋連接詞（,but）＋連接詞（as）【指由於】＋第一個子句（現在式否定句）＋連接詞（,and）＋neither＋動詞＋主詞（倒裝句）＋英文逗號（,）＋……；第二個子句。別忘了加上第二個句子，這樣才能完整敘述「由於都不會游泳，因此只能……」。

❷ 我安慰他說我也還不會游泳，並建議一同報名泳訓班。

I comforted him by telling him I couldn't swim either, and suggested that we can sign up for swimming lessons together.

| 為什麼這樣翻 2 ⋯⋯⋯⋯⋯⋯⋯⋯⋯⋯⋯⋯⋯⋯⋯⋯⋯⋯⋯⋯⋯

　　本句為過去式，表示過去已發生了的事情。**「我安慰他說我也還不會游泳」是用某一件事情來達成另一件事的意思，結構為：I（comforted him）＋by（V-ing）。括弧內可替換其他字。**「並建議一同報名泳訓班」，「that」帶領的子句（that we can sign up for swimming lessons together），是動詞「suggest」的受詞。

❶ 運動中心有游泳池,可是因為我和朋友都不會游泳。

My friend and I aren't able to swim, so even though the sports center has a swimming pool, ...

| 為什麼還能這樣翻 1 ....

　　亦可譯作,「我和朋友都不會游泳,所以即便運動中心有游泳池,……」。英文常見的寫法能將兩個連接詞寫在一起,連接接續的兩個子句。現在式主要子句(My friend and I aren't able to swim)+從屬連接詞(, so)+**連接詞(even though)**+現在式從屬子句(第一個子句(the sports center has a swimming pool)+第二個子句。這裡要留意,由於此句的連接詞為(even though),**也就是從屬連接詞,後面需要接第二個子句,句意才算完整。**

❷ 我安慰他說我也還不會游泳,並建議一同報名泳訓班。

In an effort to comfort him, I told him that neither of us could swim and suggested that we both sign up for swimming lessons.

| 為什麼還能這樣翻 2 ·······················

「我也還不會游泳」，意即「我們兩個都不會游泳」，
用「neither」表示兩者皆不會，其接續的英文敘述要用肯
定句形式，因為「neither」已是否定之意。

全文翻譯

During spring vacation, my friend and I went to the
sports center together every day. The sports center has
a swimming pool, but as my friend doesn't know how to
swim, and neither do I, we could only play squash,
tennis and use the other fitness facilities. My friend said
that he had tried to learn to swim, but he just couldn't
master it, and that's why he dispiritingly thought that he
would never swim. I comforted him by telling him I
couldn't swim either, and suggested that we can sign up
for swimming lessons together. After we asked the cost
of swimming lessons, we decided to do it and we are
determined to be able to swim before the beginning of
summer vacation.

5-4 直接受詞、間接受詞怎麼用？

關鍵技巧 活用授與動詞的句型 ▶

關鍵例句搶先看 ◉

再過一個月，就是弟弟的七歲生日，我想用自己的零用錢買禮物送他。

It will be my brother's 7th birthday next month. I want to use my pocket money to buy him a present.

基礎技巧提點

1. 間接受詞位於直接受詞之後，就使用介系詞「to」或「for」。如果間接受詞位於直接受詞之前，則不需要介系詞。

2. 不以中文標點符號為依據，需照著語意，適時斷句。

3. 英文標點符號中的分號「；」，用於連接獨立的子句。比起句號更能顯示出兩個子句之間的相關性。

4. 注意時態，動詞／be 動詞／助動詞的變化形式。

✒ **試著翻翻看**▶ **試著翻畫底線的部分**

❶ <u>再過一個月，就是弟弟的七歲生日，我想用自己的零用錢買禮物送他。</u>弟弟一直都很喜歡樂高積木（Lego），常常用積木組成很多不同形式的物體：船、飛機、城堡、機器人。

最近我發現弟弟還有另一個喜歡的東西—光劍（Lightsaber）；我認為這應該是《星際大戰》給他的啟發，而且他也說想要當「絕地武士」（Jedi）。❷ <u>我考慮買一支光劍作為他的生日禮物。</u>

❶ _____

_____

_____

❷ _____

_____

_____

❶ 再過一個月，就是弟弟的七歲生日，我想用自己的零用錢買禮物送他。

It will be my brother's 7th birthday next month. I want to use my pocket money to buy him a present.

| 為什麼這樣翻 1 ···

「再過一個月，就是弟弟的七歲生日」，是未來式文法。英文在生日的表達上，會以「第幾個生日」來表示。第一到第三為特別寫法：1st（延續至 21、31……以此類推）、2nd、3rd，其餘皆於字尾加「th」表示。

「我想用自己的零用錢買禮物送他」，是現在式文法。**「買某物給某人」，在英文有「buy（someone）something」的固定表達。此句也是用此固定句型，間接受詞（someone）位於直接受詞（something）之前，不需要介系詞。這裡間接受詞為「him」，直接受詞是「a present」**。

❷ 我考慮買一支光劍作為他的生日禮物。

I'm thinking of buying a lightsaber for him as his birthday present.

| 為什麼這樣翻 2 ··

　　「我考慮買一支光劍作為他的生日禮物」，是現在進行式。「考慮－think of」是片語，介系詞（of）後面加動名詞（V-ing）。**和上一句不同，「買某物給某人」的另外一種表達方式為：「buy something for someone」，此次間接受詞（someone）位於直接受詞（something）之後，要使用介系詞「to」或「for」**。這裡的間接受詞為「him」；直接受詞是「a lightsaber」。

　　直接受詞的意思，是指該受詞是直接隸屬於動詞的接受對象，此句「買某物給某人」，某物（something）就是買（buy）的直接受詞。

❶ 再過一個月，就是弟弟的七歲生日，我想用自己的零用錢買禮物送他。

In one month, it will be my brother's 7th birthday. I want to use my pocket money to buy a present for him.

| 為什麼還能這樣翻 1 ⋯⋯⋯⋯⋯⋯⋯⋯⋯⋯⋯⋯⋯⋯⋯⋯⋯

　　時間副詞可寫在主詞之前，本句可從「再過一個月」知道時態為未來式；亦可譯作「一個月後」，寫作「in one month's time」。間接受詞位於直接受詞之後，要用介系詞「to」或「for」連接。間接受詞（him）；直接受詞（a present）。

❷ 我考慮買一支光劍作為他的生日禮物。

I'm considering buying him a lightsaber as his birthday present.

| 為什麼還能這樣翻 2 ⋯⋯⋯⋯⋯⋯⋯⋯⋯⋯⋯⋯⋯⋯⋯⋯⋯

　　「考慮－consider」，後面的動詞要加 ing 變成動名詞。**間接受詞位於直接受詞之前，不需要介系詞**。間接受詞

（him）；直接受詞（a lightsaber）。「作為；當作－as」，是介系詞，介系詞後一定是名詞（his birthday present）。

It will be my brother's 7th birthday next month. I want to use my pocket money to buy him a present. My brother likes Lego, he often uses it to build varying objects: boats, airplanes, castles and robots.

Recently, I have realized there is another thing that my brother likes-a lightsaber; I think he got the idea from Star Wars. He also said he wants to be a "Jedi", so I'm thinking of buying a lightsaber for him as his birthday present.

如何用英文來強調語氣？

關鍵技巧

善用「附加問句」就對了 ▶

關鍵例句搶先看 ●

我們都知道，每逢中國新年假期，總是免不了塞車，對吧？

We all know that when it comes to the Chinese New Year holiday, being stuck in traffic jams is inevitable, isn't it?

基礎技巧提點

1 「交通壅塞」、「車流量大」，在英文以形容詞「heavy」來形容「交通；車流量」的壅塞情況。

2 附加問句為一個問句，或是針對已知的事再次確認。**結構：英文逗號（,）＋助動詞／be 動詞＋代名詞＋問號。**句子為肯定句的附加問句需寫成否定句；句子為否定句的附加問句，則需寫成肯定句。

3 句子為肯定句的現在式 be 動詞文法，且主詞為「I」時，附加問句需寫成「, aren't I?」。

✒ 試著翻翻看▶ 試著翻畫底線的部分

❶ 我們都知道，每逢中國新年假期，總是免不了塞車，對吧？可是今年過年期間我帶家人出遊，並沒有塞到車，想知道為什麼嗎？因為我選擇在離峰時段上路。從彰化（Changhua）開到墾丁（Kenting），車程僅三個半小時。

既然是放假期間，不像平常為了趕上班、上學，得在一定的時間出門，❷ 也就表示能避開交通壅塞的時間再上路，不是嗎？所以我強烈建議在連續假期期間出遊，應選在破曉時分出門，會讓旅途更愉快哦！

❶ _____

_____

_____

❷ _____

_____

_____

❶ 我們都知道，每逢中國新年假期，總是免不了塞車，對吧？

We all know that when it comes to the Chinese New Year holiday, being stuck in traffic jams is inevitable, isn't it?

| 為什麼這樣翻 1 ⋯⋯⋯⋯⋯⋯⋯⋯⋯⋯⋯⋯⋯⋯⋯⋯⋯

　　「塞車」是可數名詞「traffic jam」，加「s」，寫成複數形式。「總是免不了塞車，對吧？」，「塞車」是現在式被動語態（be 動詞＋動詞的過去分詞）的文法，**不定詞（to be）與動名詞（being）皆可作為句子中的主詞。以不定詞（to be）為開頭的句子通常在中文裡有「即將」的意味，而以動名詞（being）為開頭，則有狀態的意思，這裡用 being stuck 會比 to be stuck 好，因為中文裡的意涵是偏向狀態的意思。**句子為現在式 be 動詞肯定句文法，附加問句要寫成否定，配合 be 動詞「is」，寫成否定「, isn't it?」；代名詞「it」，表示「免不了塞車這件事」。

❷ 也就表示能避開交通壅塞的時間再上路，不是嗎？

..., it means that you can avoid going on the road with heavy traffic, can't you?

| 為什麼這樣翻 2 ⋯⋯⋯⋯⋯⋯⋯⋯⋯⋯⋯⋯⋯⋯⋯⋯⋯⋯⋯⋯⋯⋯⋯⋯⋯⋯⋯

　　「避開；避免」是「avoid」，其後面的動詞只能寫成動名詞形式（動詞＋ing）。**句子為現在式肯定句動詞文法，其助動詞為「can」，附加問句需寫成否定「, can't you?」。**

也可以這麼翻

❶ 我們都知道，每逢中國新年假期，總是免不了塞車，對吧？

Everyone knows that getting stuck in traffic jams is unavoidable during the Chinese New Year holiday, but is it really?

| 為什麼還能這樣翻 1 ··

依整篇文章的語意，知道其實是可避免塞車，所以**亦可解讀成「我們都知道，每逢中國新年假期，總是免不了塞車，但是真的是這樣嗎？」**。現在式文法，以主要子句（Everyone knows that getting stuck in traffic jams is unavoidable during the Chinese New Year holiday）開頭＋英文逗號（,）＋並列連接詞（but）＋主要子句疑問句（is it really?）。

❷ 也就表示能避開交通壅塞的時間再上路，不是嗎？

..., it means that it is possible to avoid traveling in heavy traffic, doesn't it?

| 為什麼還能這樣翻 2 ··

　　句子為現在式文法肯定句，主要動詞為「mean」，附加問句需使用助動詞的否定形式。附加問句結構：逗號＋助動詞（doesn't）＋代名詞（it）＋問號。附加問句用代名詞「it」，表示「is possible to avoid traveling in heavy traffic」這件事。

全文翻譯

　　We all know that when it comes to the Chinese New Year holiday, being stuck in traffic jams is inevitable, isn't it? But as I took my family out for a trip during the Chinese New Year holiday this year, we didn't have this problem. Do you want to know why? It's because I chose to get on the road at off peak time; thus, the drive from Changhua to Kenting only took 3.5 hours.

　　Since it is holiday time, not like ordinary days when you need to leave home at a certain time in order to get to work or school on time, it means that you can avoid going on the road with heavy traffic, can't you? I strongly suggest traveling right after dawn during holidays, and it will make your journey more pleasant!

Part II

英翻中
技巧

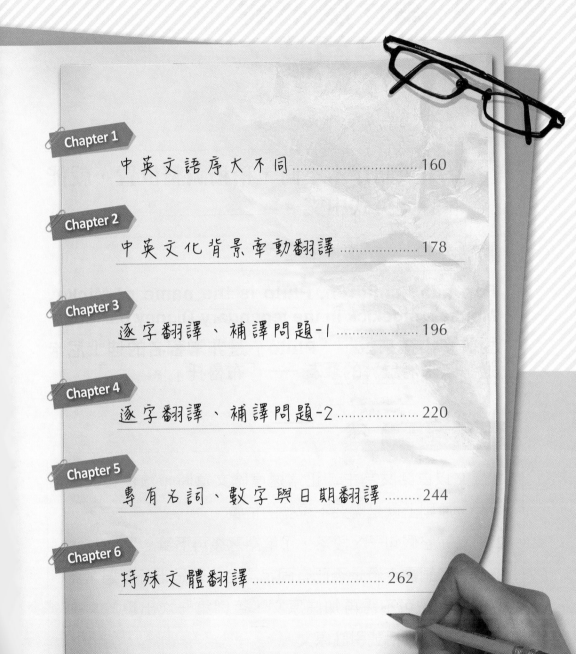

1-1 為什麼不能逐字翻譯？

中英語序本不同，稍稍調整位置，就能避免英式中文。 ▶

關鍵例句搶先看 ◗

For many children, Pluto is the name of Mickey Mouse's sidekick in the legendary Disney cartoon.

對許多小孩來說，「Pluto」是非常著名的迪士尼卡通，《米老鼠》的摯友 ── 「布魯托」。

基礎技巧提點

1 譯文以白話文為主，正常速度唸文章時，該停頓換氣時，原則上就是需要下逗號的位置。

2 需看完整個句子、段落，了解語意後再下筆。

3 專有名詞需查證是否已有固定譯名，若是十分普遍常見的譯名，可不需再加註原文，否則第一次出現於文中時，需以圓括號引註原文。

4 中文的書名號「《》」，用於電影、影集作品名稱。

✎ 試著翻翻看▶ 試著翻畫底線的部分

What is Pluto?

When you hear the name Pluto, what comes to mind?

❶ For many children, Pluto is the name of *Mickey Mouse's* sidekick in the legendary Disney cartoon.

❷ For an older generation, Pluto is the name of the ninth and final planet in our solar system. The only problem is that in 2006, following the discovery of other larger objects beyond Pluto, Pluto was downgraded to 'dwarf planet'. As a result, millions of school textbooks around the world are now outdated.

❶ _____

_____

_____

❷ _____

_____

✏ 你翻對了嗎？

❶ For many children, Pluto is the name of Mickey Mouse's sidekick in the legendary Disney cartoon.

對許多小孩來說，「Pluto」是非常著名的迪士尼卡通，《米老鼠》的摯友 ── 「布魯托」。

| **為什麼這樣翻 1** ⋯⋯⋯⋯⋯⋯⋯⋯⋯⋯⋯⋯⋯⋯⋯⋯⋯⋯⋯⋯⋯

「for＋受詞」，表示「對（某人／某事）來説」。「For many children」，是「對許多小孩來説」的意思。從上下文中，可以知道「Pluto」這個名字有不同涵意，因此需在譯文補充説明查證過後的涵意。在譯文句尾加入破折號（ ── ），用於介紹某種説法，再以單引號強調其內容。

❷ For an older generation, Pluto is the name of the ninth and final planet in our solar system.

對較年長的世代來說，「Pluto」這個名字，是在我們所屬太陽系中，最後一顆被找到的第九大行星－「冥王星」。

| 為什麼這樣翻 2 ⋯⋯⋯⋯⋯⋯⋯⋯⋯⋯⋯⋯⋯⋯⋯⋯⋯⋯⋯⋯

　　「for＋受詞」，表示「對（某人／某事）來說」。依文意查證專有名詞「Pluto」在太陽系中的譯名為：「冥王星」；句尾加入破折號（ ─ ），用於介紹某種說法，再以單引號（「」）強調其內容。翻譯時，譯文要符合中文語序，先敘述地點（太陽系中），才接後續的敘述。也要在不更改原意的前提下，適時加入譯出文，使譯文流暢。

❶ For many children, Pluto is the name of Mickey Mouse's sidekick in the legendary Disney cartoon.

「Pluto」這個名字對許多小孩來說，代表著名迪士尼卡通《米老鼠》的好朋友。

| 為什麼還能這樣翻 1 ....

在不更改原意且譯文通暢的情況下，本句譯可亦作「「Pluto」這個名字對許多小孩來說，代表著名迪士尼卡通《米老鼠》的好朋友」。**請避免逐字翻成：對很多小孩來說，「Pluto」是《米老鼠》的好朋友在著名的迪士尼卡通裡。**

❷ For an older generation, Pluto is the name of the ninth and final planet in our solar system.

「Pluto」這個名字在年長一點的人心中，代表的是「冥王星」－太陽系中最後一顆被找到的第九大行星。

| 為什麼還能這樣翻 2 ....

本句也可將「For an older generation」，譯作「對年長一點的人來說」，但不可誤譯成「上一個世代；老一輩」，

因為原文並無明確指明是「last generation」，而是依上一段敘述做出的對比，泛指比現在小孩還要年長的所有人。此句亦可譯作，「「Pluto」這個名字在年長一點的人心中，代表的是「冥王星」－太陽系中最後一顆被找到的第九大行星。」。

全文翻譯

「Pluto」是什麼？

當你聽到「Pluto」這個名字的時候，會想到什麼？

對許多小孩來說，「Pluto」是非常著名的迪士尼卡通，《米老鼠》的摯友－「布魯托」。

對較年長的世代來說，「Pluto」這個名字，是在我們所屬太陽系中，最後一顆被找到的第九大行星－「冥王星」。唯一的問題是，隨著二〇〇六年發現了其他比「冥王星」更大的行星之後，「冥王星」就被降格成「矮行星」（dwarf planet）。結果導致全世界數百萬計的教科書，全成了過時的書籍。

1-2 When 子句的中譯順序該放「前」或「後」？

關鍵技巧 英翻中時，放入「中文的邏輯思考」 ▶

關鍵例句搶先看 ●

I always feel so much better when I start the day with a good workout.

每當我以充分的運動做為一天的開始時，身體總是感覺好很多。

基礎技巧提點

1 翻譯時，為了文章流暢度，以及譯文的完整性，需適時在不更改原意的前提下，加入譯出文。

2 通常第二人稱的表示方式是「你」，而這個「你」就是泛指讀者。

3 表時間的連接詞 when／after／before ，其英文結構為：主要子句＋when／before／after＋附屬子句。**中文譯文要將連接詞與附屬子句先譯出，再譯出主要子句，才符合中文語意。**

✏️ 試著翻翻看 ▶ 試著翻畫底線的部分

I often go swimming in the morning before work. ❶ <u>You shouldn't eat just before you swim, so I always have breakfast after I come out of the pool.</u>

Swimming is a good exercise. It keeps me fit ❷, and I <u>always feel so much better when I start the day with a good workout.</u> It is best to learn to swim when you are a child. Besides its health benefits, it is important for everyone to learn how to swim because you never know when it might just save your life.

❶ _____

_____

_____

❷ _____

_____

❶ You shouldn't eat just before you swim, so I always have breakfast after I come out of the pool.

你不該在游泳的前一刻吃東西，所以我總是在游泳後吃早餐。

| 為什麼這樣翻 1 ···

「just before」，不得略過重點字「just」，譯作「前不久；前一刻」。本文以第二人稱「you」，泛指看這篇文章的所有人。表時間的連接詞 when／after／before ，其英文結構為：主要子句＋when／before／after＋附屬子句。

中文譯文要將連接詞與附屬子句先譯出（所以我總是在游泳後），再譯出主要子句（吃早餐），才符合中文語意。

❷ ..., and I always feel so much better when I start the day with a good workout.

每當我以充分的運動做為一天的開始時，身體總是感覺好很多。

| 為什麼這樣翻 2

「I always feel so much better」，依前後文的敘述，得知是覺得「身體狀況」好很多的意思。**中文譯文需補充說明所指為何，不可只以逐字譯出的方式**，譯作「我總是覺得好很多」，會讓人摸不著頭緒是在表示有關哪方面的事。表時間的連接詞 when／after／before，**中文譯文要將連接詞與附屬子句先譯出（每當我以充分的運動做為一天的開始時），再譯出主要子句（身體總是感覺好很多）**。

❶ You shouldn't eat just before you swim, so I always have breakfast after I come out of the pool.

你不該在吃完東西後馬上游泳，所以我總是游完後才吃早餐。

| 為什麼還能這樣翻 1 ⋯⋯⋯⋯⋯⋯⋯⋯⋯⋯⋯⋯⋯⋯⋯⋯⋯⋯

「你不該在游泳的前一刻吃東西」，亦可譯作「你不該在吃完東西後馬上游泳」，不影響原意。「所以我總是在游泳後」，亦可譯作「游完後」。**唯其中文譯文仍需將連接詞與附屬子句先譯出（你不該在吃完東西後馬上游泳），再譯出主要子句（所以我總是游完才吃早餐）。譯文需符合中文語序的因果關係，亦可譯作「我總是在游完泳後才吃早餐，因為游泳前不該吃東西」。**

❷ ..., and I always feel so much better when I start the day with a good workout.

只要我在一天的開始好好地運動一番，我的身體總是會感覺好很多。

｜為什麼還能這樣翻 2

　　中文譯文要將連接詞與附屬子句先譯出（只要我在一天的開始好好地運動一番），再譯出主要子句（我的身體總是會感覺好很多）。「a good workout」，亦可譯作「適度的運動；好好地運動一番」。

全文翻譯

　　我常在早上上班前游泳。你不該在游泳的前一刻吃東西，所以我總是在游泳後吃早餐。

　　游泳是一項好的運動，讓我保持健康。每當我以充分的運動做為一天的開始時，身體總是感覺好很多。最好是從小就開始學游泳，況且游泳對健康有益。對每個人來說，會游泳是很重要的，因為你不知道何時可能派上用場，救自己一命。

中譯文似乎完全和英文對不起來，為什麼呢？

這招一定要學會：「先找出該句子、段落的主詞，以符合中文語序的方式譯出。」！ ▶

關鍵例句搶先看 ◐

By beating more than fifty other entrants, the girl, whose mother says she has preserved and never given up, shows that practice really does make perfect.

女孩的母親表示，能勝過其他五十多名參賽者，靠的是女兒永不放棄的精神，以及持續練習。這證明了熟能生巧的道理。

基礎技巧提點

1. 英文語法將時間、地方置於句子最後，但中文語序會在句中先說明時間和地點，譯文需符合中文語法。

2. 譯文前後連貫性與流暢度需符合中文語法，不能逐字譯，需視全文語意，適當省略主詞譯文，或加入譯出文。

✎ **試著翻翻看▶** **試著翻畫底線的部分**

❶ A seven-year-old girl without hands has won a national handwriting competition in the US. The girl, born with no hands, does not use prosthetics. She has to stand in order to get the right angle to write and holds the pencil between her arms. Her principal describes her as "an inspiration" and "someone who never lets anything get in her way". ❷ By beating more than fifty other entrants, the girl, whose mother says she has preserved and never given up, shows that practice really does make perfect.

❶ _____

_____

_____

❷ _____

_____

_____

❶ A seven-year-old girl without hands has won a national handwriting competition in the US.

美國一名沒有雙手的七歲女孩，贏得全國書寫比賽冠軍。

| 為什麼這樣翻 1 ·····································

比賽／競賽用「win」來表示贏得某種比賽，意即獲得冠軍的意思。**中文語序會先說明時間和地方，因此不可依英文語序直譯為「一名沒有雙手的七歲女孩，贏得全國書寫比賽冠軍，在美國。」**譯文既不通順，亦不符合中文語法。

❷ By beating more than fifty other entrants, the girl, whose mother says she has preserved and never given up, shows that practice really does make perfect.

女孩的母親表示，能勝過其他五十多名參賽者，靠的是女兒永不放棄的精神，以及持續練習。這證明了熟能生巧的道理。

| 為什麼這樣翻 2 ⋯⋯⋯⋯⋯⋯⋯⋯⋯⋯⋯⋯⋯⋯⋯⋯⋯⋯

下筆前，先找出該句子、段落的主詞，以符合中文語序的方式譯出。

「practice really does make perfect」，是將英文諺語「practice makes perfect」，寫成強調驗證此諺語的說法，而諺語是從日常生活中的體會，不但具教育義意，更代表古老智慧的流傳，**所以在譯出文加上「道理」兩字，會比僅譯作「熟能生巧」，更能表示出諺語的作用。**

❶ A seven-year-old girl without hands has won a national handwriting competition in the US.

美國一名沒有雙手的七歲女孩，奪下全國書寫比賽冠軍。

| 為什麼還能這樣翻 1 ⋯⋯⋯⋯⋯⋯⋯⋯⋯⋯⋯⋯⋯⋯⋯⋯⋯⋯

　　「in the US」，除了翻作「美國（的）女孩」，將「in the US」英文的時間副詞，**轉化為中文的形容詞**外，亦可譯作「在美國一名」，並將「在」省略，**讓語句更通順，符合中文**。「won a national handwriting competition」，的「won」亦可譯作「奪下；奪得」，讓本句的文字情緒，更顯得激昂，與前句的「沒有雙手的七歲女孩」，構成令人振奮的語氣。

❷ By beating more than fifty other entrants, the girl, whose mother says she has preserved and never given up, shows that practice really does make perfect.

女孩的母親說：「能勝過其他五十多名參賽者，全是因為她永不放棄的精神，並且持續的練習。這個例子，驗證了熟能生巧的道理。」

| 為什麼還能這樣翻 2

「shows that practice really does make perfect」，還可譯作「這證明了多練習，真的能達到熟能生巧的結果」。本段譯文是女孩母親表達的敘述，表示這件事因此亦可以在原文沒有以引述人物言語的呈現下，在譯文中，以冒號加單引號，將敘述內容以第一人稱方式譯出。

全文翻譯

　　美國一名沒有雙手的七歲女孩，贏得全國書寫比賽冠軍。女孩一出生便無雙手，也沒有使用義肢。她以雙臂夾住鉛筆，而且必須保持站姿，才能找到正確的角度寫字。學校校長形容她是個「鼓舞人心」、「絕不向任何阻撓低頭」的人。女孩的母親表示，能勝過其他五十多名參賽者，靠的是女兒永不放棄的精神，以及持續練習。這證明了熟能生巧的道理。

2-1 「A bucket list」可以直接翻成「一張水桶清單」嗎？

先了解英文片語、慣用語的意義，中文譯文才能更貼切。 ▶

關鍵例句搶先看 ◯

A bucket list is a list of things that you hope to do in your final years, or in other words before you die.

「a bucket list」（「死前的待辦清單」）即你希望在死前完成的事情清單。

基礎技巧提點

1 不可省略或誤譯重點文字，更不可更改原意。

2 需在了解英文的片語、慣語涵意後，再以最貼切的中文譯出，不可以片面字意譯出。「a bucket list」—死前的待辦清單；「to kick the bucket」—死掉；翹辮子。

3 需先看完整個句子、段落，再下筆。內容為解釋特定字詞語意時，在單引號「「」」內呈現原文，強調其內容，先不直接譯出中文意思。

試著翻翻看 ▶ 試著翻畫底線的部分

Recently a new English term has become common. ❶ A bucket list is a list of things that you hope to do in your final years, or in other words before you die. The term arises from the idiom to kick the bucket which means to die.

❷ The idea was popularized by the 2007 movie *The Bucket List*, but it is now not limited to the old. Recently the young have started using the term to represent lifetime goals. A bucket list can include anything from raising a family to climbing a mountain or sailing a boat around the world.

What's on your bucket list?

❶ _____

_____

_____

❷ _____

_____

❶ A bucket list is a list of things that you hope to do in your final years, or in other words before you die.

──「a bucket list」（「死前的待辦清單」）即你希望在死前完成的事情清單。

| 為什麼這樣翻 1 ·······························

　　英文呈現特別強調特定字詞的方式有兩種：粗體字、單引號。中文以單引號（「」）表示強調內容。整篇文章架構中，稍後馬上解釋了「a bucket list」涵意，因此第一次出現時，以破折號加單引號和原文的方式呈現，並以圓括弧加單引號和譯文補充說明，會讓整篇文章主述的重點與文意，更加鮮明。

❷ The idea was popularized by the 2007 movie *The Bucket List*, but it is now not limited to the old.

二〇〇七年的《一路玩到掛》（*The Bucket List*）電影，大力宣揚了這個列出死前待辦清單的構想，但現在，這已不是只有年長者才會做的事。

| 為什麼這樣翻 2 ⋯⋯⋯⋯⋯⋯⋯⋯⋯⋯⋯⋯⋯⋯⋯⋯⋯⋯

書名號內的電影名稱以固有譯文表示，但為求完整，建議將原文以斜體字附註在圓括弧內。**將時間擺在敘述事情的前面，譯文較為通暢，並符合中文語法。**

「was popularized」是被動語態文法，但在中文譯文不需強調被動的狀態，也就是不需翻成「被大力宣揚」。

❶ A bucket list is a list of things that you hope to do in your final years, or in other words before you die.

「A bucket list」－是在生命的最後幾年，想完成的事情清單；換句話說，也就是在你死掉之前，想要做的事。

| 為什麼還能這樣翻 1 ⋯⋯⋯⋯⋯⋯⋯⋯⋯⋯⋯⋯⋯⋯⋯⋯⋯⋯⋯⋯⋯⋯⋯⋯⋯⋯

可以用破折號（ ── ），表示解釋的意思。用分號表示兩個句子之間的相關性。「before you die」雖然在字面上只有「在你死掉之前」的意思。「hope to do」中文雖馬上會直譯成「希望去做」，但在這裡翻成「想要做的事」會更好。

❷ The idea was popularized by the 2007 movie *The Bucket List*, but it is now not limited to the old.

二〇〇七年的《一路玩到掛》（*The Bucket List*）電影，宣揚了這個列出死前待辦清單的構想。況且現在，不是只有年長者才會這麼做。

| 為什麼還能這樣翻 2 ⋯⋯⋯⋯⋯⋯⋯⋯⋯⋯⋯⋯⋯⋯⋯⋯⋯⋯⋯

「but it is now not limited to the old」，依文章前後語意，亦可譯作「況且現在，這不只是年長者的專利」；「而且，現在的年輕人也會這麼做」，只要文意正確、通暢即可。但不適合再將英文代名詞的「it」，譯成「列出死前待辦清單」，會讓譯文過於冗長，此部分已清楚其所指為何，故直接以「這；這麼做」表示即可。

全文翻譯

近來，一個新的英文專門名詞，變得十分常見 ——「a bucket list」（「死前的待辦清單」）；即你希望在死前完成的事情清單。這個專門名詞是從英文慣用語：「to kick the bucket」（死掉；翹辮子）衍生而來。

二〇〇七年的《一路玩到掛》（*The Bucket List*）電影，大力宣揚了這個列出死前待辦清單的構想，但現在，這已不是只有年長者才會做的事。近來，年輕人開始以這個專門名詞，代表擬定有生之年想達成的目標清單。死前待辦清單的內容包羅萬象，從養兒育女到登山，或是乘帆船環遊世界都有。

你的清單會是什麼呢？

2-2 「In one ear and out the other」怎麼翻？

關鍵技巧 「耳邊風」vs.「一耳進，一耳出」▶

關鍵例句搶先看 ●

It often seems that with children, everything you tell them goes in one ear and out the other.

父母對小孩說的話，似乎常被他們當耳邊風。

基礎技巧提點

1 英文常以代名詞／指示代名詞／名詞在文中代替主詞或
受詞連貫敘述，譯文需適時於不容易了解所指為何時，
將其完整主詞或受詞譯出。

2 英文慣用語，應依其意涵，譯為符合其意的中文成語。
英文慣用語「in one ear and out the other」，即中文成
語「耳邊風」。

3 譯為成語的內文，若有含數字在其中，需以中文字譯
出，不得以阿拉伯數字代替。

✏️ 試著翻翻看 ▶ 試著翻畫底線的部分

It's not easy to raise a child. Parenting magazines make it all look so simple, but the day-to-day reality of trying to be a good parent is something completely different.

Let me tell you a little about my experiences. ❶ I have two sons. They often argue with each other, and both of them always want to win or to be first to do something. They need to learn that in life working together is often the best option.

❷ It often seems that with children, everything you tell them goes in one ear and out the other. In my experience, it is always best to get children to repeat instructions back to you to be sure that they are listening.

❶ _____

_____

❷ _____

_____

❶ I have two sons. They often argue with each other, and both of them always want to win or to be first to do something.

我有兩個兒子，他們不時爭吵，而且總是想贏過對方或是搶著做某事。

| 為什麼這樣翻 1 ⋯⋯⋯⋯⋯⋯⋯⋯⋯⋯⋯⋯⋯⋯⋯⋯⋯⋯⋯⋯⋯

「They often argue with each other」，不以逐字譯成「他們不時彼此互相爭吵」，僅以中文「他們不時爭吵」，便能充分表現出是彼此爭吵的意境。

「and both of them always...」，因為前句與本句敘述主角為「我的兩個兒子／他們」，故不需再譯出「他們兩個人……」，只接續敘述，也就是「而且總是……」，避免譯文重覆且過於冗長。

❷ It often seems that with children, everything you tell them goes in one ear and out the other.

父母對小孩說的話，似乎常被他們當耳邊風。

| 為什麼這樣翻 2 ·······

「... everything you tell them...」，其中的代名詞主詞「you」，是泛指「父母們」；**為了譯文能充分表現出其所指為何，在這裡將代名詞譯回主詞名詞－「父母對小孩說的話」**。其受詞「them」，在語意明確情況下，直接用代名詞「他們」表示。**英文慣用語：「in one ear and out the other」，與成語「耳邊風」的意境最為貼切。**

❶ I have two sons. They often argue with each other, and both of them always want to win or to be first to do something.

我有兩個兒子；他們時常爭吵，也常想打敗對方或是搶著做某事。

| 為什麼還能這樣翻 1 ⋯⋯⋯⋯⋯⋯⋯⋯⋯⋯⋯⋯⋯⋯⋯⋯⋯⋯⋯⋯⋯⋯

　　分號「；」，在中文裡用於連接獨立的句子。顯示出句子之間的相關性。「win」在本文是「打敗；勝過」的意思，而不是「贏得（某）獎品」的意思。

❷ It often seems that with children, everything you tell them goes in one ear and out the other.

小孩子對父母的吩咐，總是一耳進，一耳出似地。

| 為什麼還能這樣翻 2 ⋯⋯⋯⋯⋯⋯⋯⋯⋯⋯⋯⋯⋯⋯⋯⋯⋯⋯⋯⋯⋯⋯

　　「... everything you tell them...」，譯文可將「小孩」作為主詞，直接敘述小孩對父母的（話）吩咐所抱持的態度。英文慣用語「in one ear and out the other」，若以白話文直譯，亦能表達其意涵。**可打趣似地譯作「左耳進，右耳**

出」，或是「右耳進，左耳出」，較客觀的直譯文是「一耳進，一耳出」。

全文翻譯

養育小孩可是一點也不容易。親子教養雜誌，總讓教養小孩這件事，看起來像是件再簡單不過的事，但是在日常現實生活中試著當好父母，卻完全不是這麼一回事。

讓我來告訴你一點自己的經驗。我有兩個兒子，他們不時爭吵，而且總是想贏過對方或是搶著做某事。他們需要學習，合作常是生活中最好的選項。

父母對小孩說的話，似乎常被他們當耳邊風。以我的經驗，最好是要小孩重覆一遍你的吩咐，才能確保他們有聽進去。

「Miss the boat」翻成「錯過船班」，正確嗎？

關鍵技巧 譯文正確很重要，但更要細查上下文，才能翻出通順的譯文！ ▶

關鍵例句搶先看 ◉

Waiting for that extra 10-20% certainty may mean missing the boat.

遲遲無法下決定，就為了等待多百分之十至二十的確定性，意味著錯失良機的可能。

基礎技巧提點

1 英文常用代名詞／指示代名司／名詞，在文章中連貫敘述，需適時在譯文中將代名詞，換成主詞譯出。

2 英文慣用語「miss the boat」，意同中文成語「錯失良機」。

3 依照全文語意，可判定哪些敘述為英文慣用語，需查證其涵意，不以逐字方式直譯，並套以最貼近的中文成語或解釋。

試著翻畫底線的部分

The seventy percent rule: Your life might be changed for the better by applying the 70% rule. ❶ From business to study, we could all benefit from this idea that originated in the military. It says that in order to make a decision you only need to be 70% certain. Effective leaders never wait longer than this before they act.

Soldiers regularly have to make decisions with limited information and time, and real life is just the same. Managers are often faced with this situation on a daily basis. ❷ Waiting for that extra 10-20% certainty may mean missing the boat. So stop procrastinating, make a decision and get your life moving.

❶ _____

_____

_____

❷ _____

_____

❶ From business to study, we could all benefit from this idea that originated in the military. It says that in order to make a decision you only need to be 70% certain.

從出社會到求學，我們都能從這起源於軍事的概念中獲益。這個守則是說：做出決策，只需百分之七十的確定性。

| 為什麼這樣翻 1 ⋯⋯⋯⋯⋯⋯⋯⋯⋯⋯⋯⋯⋯⋯⋯⋯⋯⋯⋯

　　「From business to study」，英文以這兩個部分，做為人生中的重要歷程，即「出社會工作和求學」。冒號「：」可用於解釋。「It says that...」，其代名詞「it」，指的是「this idea」；而「this idea」指的是上一段敘述中的「the 70% rule」。譯文不直譯作「它是說：⋯⋯」，以「這個守則是說：⋯⋯」的譯法，較能充分表達其所指為何。

❷ Waiting for that extra 10-20% certainty may mean missing the boat.

遲遲無法下決定，就為了等待多百分之十至二十的確定性，意味著錯失良機的可能。

| 為什麼這樣翻 2 ·······

　　此句依據全文意涵，補充譯文「遲遲無法下決定」，與最後一段的「所以請別再拖延，做好決定」（原文：So stop procrastinating, make a decision and get your life moving.）相呼應。「... may mean missing the boat」，語意有預設與假定性質的猜測，**故將「mean」譯作「意味著」。不能直譯為「錯過船班」，依照前後文，很明顯此為英文慣用語，代表其特定寓意「錯失良機」，要小心誤譯的情形。**

❶ From business to study, we could all benefit from this idea that originated in the military. It says that in order to make a decision you only need to be 70% certain.

從工作到仍屬求學階段的我們，都能從這起源於軍事的概念中獲益。這個守則是說：做出決策，只需 70%的確定性。

| 為什麼還能這樣翻 1 ·····························

　　「從出社會到求學」，可在不影響原意的情況下，在譯文中加入「階段」。「百分之七十」，亦可以阿拉伯數字和符號譯作「70%」。

❷ Waiting for that extra 10-20% certainty may mean missing the boat.

等待多 10%～20%的確定性，也許意味著有錯失良機的可能。

| 為什麼還能這樣翻 2 ·····························

　　本段譯文若僅以英文字義上的意思譯作「等待多10%～20%的確定性」，譯文仍屬完整，且不影響原意與文

章結構。百分比的表示方式可用阿拉伯數字和符號譯出。「may mean」，亦可譯作「也許意味著……的可能」。

全文翻譯

百分之七十守則

運用百分之七十守則，也許能讓你的生活變得更美好。從出社會到求學，我們都能從這起源於軍事的概念中獲益。這個守則是說：做出決策，只需百分之七十的確定性。有效率的領導者，絕不等到超過百分之七十的確定性後，才有所行動。

軍人經常必須在有限的資訊與時間下，做出決策，而現實生活中，也正是如此。擔任管理層級職位的人，每日常需面對這種情況。遲遲無法下決定，就為了等待多百分之十至二十的確定性，意味著錯失良機的可能。所以請別再蹉跎，做好決定，讓生活向前邁進。

3-1 「With」只能翻「隨著」嗎？

關鍵技巧 善用中文思維，你還有更好的翻法！ ▶

關鍵例句搶先看 ◑

With all the distractions of modern life, most teenagers stay up late, so getting enough sleep to not affect school the next day is not easy.

現代的生活，有太多讓人分心的事，多數青少年有晚睡的情形，所以要睡眠充足又不影響隔天上學，實在很難。

基礎技巧提點

1 英文語法與中文語法不同，需在看完整個句子、段落，了解文意後再譯出。

2 「like」有兩個意思：做動詞用—「喜歡」；做介系詞用—「像」。

3 專業術語／名詞的譯名需查證。「biology」有「生理學；生理」的意思，若是用於形容人類作習，則需譯作「生理習性」較為恰當。

✏️ 試著翻翻看 ▶ 試著翻畫底線的部分

How much sleep do teenagers need?

Waking up for school in the morning is not easy for most teenagers.

❶ With all the distractions of modern life, most teenagers stay up late, so getting enough sleep to not affect school the next day is not easy.

The problem is made worse by biology. Teenagers need more sleep, but are programmed to go to sleep later and get up later. ❷ Asking a teenager to get up at 7am is like asking a six-year-old to get up at 5am. Maybe schools should start class later in the morning to allow their students to get more sleep.

❶ _____

_____

❷ _____

_____

① With all the distractions of modern life, most teenagers stay up late, so getting enough sleep to not affect school the next day is not easy.

現代的生活，有太多讓人分心的事，多數青少年有晚睡的情形，所以要睡眠充足又不影響隔天上學，實在很難。

| 為什麼這樣翻 1 ⋯⋯⋯⋯⋯⋯⋯⋯⋯⋯⋯⋯⋯⋯⋯⋯⋯⋯⋯⋯⋯⋯⋯⋯⋯⋯⋯⋯⋯

在看完整個句子後，以符合中文語法的譯文，從「With all the distractions of modern life」來看，以先說明「在何時」有太多讓人分心的事，使譯文語序通順，即「現在的生活」。

「not easy」，直譯為「不容易」的意思，也可視譯文流暢度，直接翻作「難」。

在不更改原意的情況下適時加入譯文，使譯文更具完整性，譯作「多數青少年有晚睡的情形」，會比直譯作「多數青少年晚睡」更好。

❷ Asking a teenager to get up at 7am is like asking a six-year-old to get up at 5am.

要青少年早上七點起床，就像是要一個六歲小孩在早上五點起床般地困難。

| 為什麼這樣翻 2 ⋯⋯⋯⋯⋯⋯⋯⋯⋯⋯⋯⋯⋯⋯⋯⋯⋯⋯⋯⋯

　　英文「like」因詞性的不同，有兩種全然不同的意思：動詞指「喜歡」；介系詞為「像」，而這兩種用法皆十分常用，需依原文文法與語意，避免誤譯的可能。

　　「ask」在本句是「要求」的意思，配合後續內容語意，譯文僅以「要」，即能表示「要求」的意涵，並補充「困難」兩字的譯文，與上一段內容中的「not easy」相呼應。

❶ With all the distractions of modern life, most teenagers stay up late, so getting enough sleep to not affect school the next day is not easy.

現代生活中，存在著太多讓人分心的事，使得大部分青少年有晚睡情形，因此想要有充足的睡眠又不影響隔天上學，並不容易。

| 為什麼還能這樣翻 1 ⋯⋯⋯⋯⋯⋯⋯⋯⋯⋯⋯⋯⋯⋯⋯⋯⋯⋯

　　只要在不更改原意的前提下，譯文能不同的中文用字，詮譯相同意思。「not easy」，直譯為「不容易」亦可。「most teenagers」，可譯作「多數青少年；大部分青少年；大多數青少年；絕大多數的青少年；絕大部分的青少年」，皆為正確。

❷ Asking a teenager to get up at 7am is like asking a six-year-old to get up at 5am.

要求青少年早上 7 點起床，就像是要求 6 歲的小孩早上 5 點起床一樣。

| 為什麼還能這樣翻 2

表示時間與年齡的數值，皆可以阿拉伯數字代替。譯文依句子語意譯出後，並未補充與前段句子可相呼應的文字，如「困難」，在這並不影響其譯文完整性，但是否補充譯出文，仍需視譯文的完整性與流暢程度而定。

全文翻譯

青少年需要多少睡眠？

對大多數青少年來說，早上起床上學，並不是件容易的事。

現代的生活，有太多讓人分心的事，多數青少年有晚睡的情形，所以要睡眠充足又不影響隔天上學，實在很難。

生理習性又讓這個問題更糟。青少年需要更長的睡眠，但卻養成晚睡晚起的習慣。要青少年早上七點起床，就像是要一個六歲小孩在早上五點起床般地困難。也許學校應該把第一節課安排在早上稍晚的時間，讓學生能睡久一點。

這句英文沒有「世上」這兩字，多翻沒有問題嗎？

關鍵技巧 適時補上譯文，會比單純譯出「相信有鬼魂」更為完整。 ▶

關鍵例句搶先看 ▶

Do you believe in ghosts, the supernatural or alien abduction?

你相信世上有鬼魂、超自然力量，或是外星人綁架事件嗎？

基礎技巧提點

1 譯其意，不同的意境與內容下，會有不同的用字與表達方式。翻譯時，為了流暢度，並有助讀者充分了解文章要表達的意思，可在不更改原意的前提下，適時加入譯出文。

2 英文片語「on the other hand」，意即「另一方面」。

3 專業術語／名詞的譯名需查證，本文敘述層面為探討超自然為主軸，「alien abduction」已有固有的「外星人綁架」譯名。

✏ 試著翻翻看 ▶ **試著翻畫底線的部分**

❶ Do you believe in ghosts, the supernatural or alien abduction?

It turns out that what people believe is greatly influenced by where they live. Alien abduction is a common belief in the US. In Europe, it is considered weird, while few in Asia have even heard of it. ❷ On the other hand, belief in the existence of ghosts is an accepted part of the culture in many countries in the Far East; however, few westerners believe that they are real.

❶ _____

_____

_____

❷ _____

_____

_____

❶ Do you believe in ghosts, the supernatural or alien abduction?

你相信世上有鬼魂、超自然力量，或是外星人綁架事件嗎？

| 為什麼這樣翻 1 ⋯⋯⋯⋯⋯⋯⋯⋯⋯⋯⋯⋯⋯⋯⋯⋯⋯⋯⋯⋯⋯⋯⋯⋯

英文語法中，敘述多項事物時，會以英文逗號「,」區隔不同元素或概念，直至以「or／and」連接最後一項敘述事物。

而在中文譯文中，敘述多項事物時，以頓號「、」區隔不同元素或概念，並在連接最後一項敘述事物時，以逗號「,」區隔。

「Do you believe in ghosts...」，適時在譯文加上「世上」不影響原意，且會比單純譯出「相信有鬼魂」更為完整。

❷ On the other hand, belief in the existence of ghosts is an accepted part of the culture in many countries in the Far East; however, few westerners believe that they are real.

以另一方面來看，遠東地區許多國家的文化，皆相信世上有鬼魂的存在，不過卻很少有西方人相信鬼魂真實存在。

| 為什麼這樣翻 2 ┈┈┈┈┈┈┈┈┈┈┈┈┈┈┈┈┈┈┈┈┈

　　為了讓上下文更有連貫性，以符合語意的方式，在「on the other hand」的譯文加上「以……來看」。英文語法結構是將地方，放在句子最後，**但譯文需符合中文語法，也就是先說明地方，再敘述其他相關事件。**

　　英文語法中，副詞當連接詞時，需以分號（ ; ）＋副詞（ however ）＋逗號（ , ）表示。中文譯文不需配合英文標點符號的使用，只依照符合中文語法的方式標註標點符號。

❶ Do you believe in ghosts, the supernatural or alien abduction?

你相信鬼魂、超自然力量、外星人綁架,真實存在嗎?

| 為什麼還能這樣翻 1 ⋯⋯⋯⋯⋯⋯⋯⋯⋯⋯⋯⋯⋯⋯⋯

　　可用頓號「、」,區隔成列的不同元素或概念,最後總結時,以逗號區隔結尾敘述。

❷ On the other hand, belief in the existence of ghosts is an accepted part of the culture in many countries in the Far East; however, few westerners believe that they are real.

以另一方面來看,遠東地區許多國家的文化,具備了相信鬼魂存在的信念,然而相信鬼魂真實存在的西方人卻不多。

| 為什麼還能這樣翻 2 ⋯⋯⋯⋯⋯⋯⋯⋯⋯⋯⋯⋯⋯⋯⋯

　　「皆相信世上有鬼魂的存在」,其原文為「belief in the existence of ghosts is an accepted part...」。亦可譯作「文化」中「具備」的某種特質;將名詞「belief」,做為其文

化所具備的特質，譯作「具備了相信鬼魂存在的信念」。
「很少」，亦可譯作「不多」。

全文翻譯

　　你相信世上有鬼魂、超自然力量，或是外星人綁架事件嗎？

　　結果發現，居住地對人會相信什麼樣的事件，有極大的影響。在美國，普遍相信有外星人綁架人類的事件。在歐洲，會認為這是一種怪誕的想法，而在亞洲，很多人幾乎連聽都沒聽過。以另一方面來看，遠東地區許多國家的文化，皆相信世上有鬼魂的存在，不過卻很少有西方人相信鬼魂真實存在。

3-3 「with their eyes glued to their cellphones」，不能直譯為「眼睛黏在手機上」嗎？

關鍵技巧 這樣翻雖然正確，但你還有更簡潔、流暢的譯法！ ▶

關鍵例句搶先看 ◐

Don't you think many people spend too much time with their eyes glued to their cellphones?

你不認為很多人花太多時間滑手機嗎？

基礎技巧提點

1 因時代、科技而衍生出的約定成俗字詞用語，需視譯文內容，適時附以註解。「eyes glued to their cellphones」，在譯文中若是動詞形式，可譯作「滑手機」；若是名詞或形容詞形式，可譯作「低頭族」。

2 英文以縮寫形式表示時，需依文章內容，判定其正確全名後，再查證譯名。「P.S.」也能寫成「PS」、「PS.」，或作小寫型態。可能用於表示「每秒」、「一兆分之一秒」，或是「附言」。

✏ **試著翻翻看** ▶ **試著翻畫底線的部分**

❶ Don't you think many people spend spend too much time with their eyes glued to their cellphones? If you are in a public place now, look up and around you. Chances are that almost everyone near you is staring at a little screen in their own world. And it's not only the young. It seems that only the elderly are still interacting with the real world around them. ❷ So why not give your eyes a break and speak to the person next to you?

P.S. If you are reading this on a mobile device, then you are forgiven.

❶ _____

_____

_____

❷ _____

_____

❶ Don't you think many people spend too much time with their eyes glued to their cellphones?

你不認為很多人花太多時間滑手機嗎？

| 為什麼這樣翻 1 ⋯⋯⋯⋯⋯⋯⋯⋯⋯⋯⋯⋯⋯⋯⋯⋯⋯⋯⋯⋯

　　英文的否定疑問句，其語意為肯定的意思，意即這段話的語意表示「很多人花太多時間滑手機」。「with their eyes glued to their cellphones」，若採直譯為「眼睛黏在手機上」，譯文仍可理解，但不夠簡潔、流暢。**以「滑手機」一詞，更能貼切地形容這句話的意境**，是在智慧型手機問世後，才開始出現的用詞，用於表示使用智慧型手機眾多功能的狀態。

❷ So why not give your eyes a break and speak to the person next to you?

何不讓你的眼睛休息一下，轉而跟身旁的人交談？

| 為什麼這樣翻 2

　　為了譯文流暢度，有時需適時加入不影響原意的譯出文，替句子稍作潤飾，會使句子更加圓潤。本句為否定疑問句，其意境為肯定的涵意，加入譯出文「轉而」，與前句表示目前眼睛處疲勞使用狀態的「讓眼睛休息一下」，形成對比並帶入下一句譯文「跟身旁的人交談」。

❶ Don't you think many people spend too much time with their eyes glued to their cellphones?

你不覺得很多人花太多時間，盯著手機螢幕看嗎？

| 為什麼還能這樣翻 1 ···

　　若譯出文並非僅供台灣使用，或者並無使用「滑手機」或「低頭族」的新形態字詞時，譯文應僅以完整句意譯作「盯著手機螢幕看」，以免造成誤解。

❷ So why not give your eyes a break and speak to the person next to you?

所以，不妨讓你的雙眼休息一下，跟身邊的人聊天？

| 為什麼還能這樣翻 2 ···

　　「何不；眼睛」，亦可譯作「不妨；雙眼」，意思皆相同。「身旁；交談」，亦可譯作「身邊；聊天」，意思皆相同。無加入譯出文修飾的句子，只要句子要表達的意思清楚，即屬正確譯文，是否需要刻意潤飾，需視譯文用途而定。

全文翻譯

你不認為很多人花太多時間滑手機嗎？若你正身處公共場所，請環顧四周。會看到的，幾乎都是兩眼直盯著小螢幕，沉浸在自己世界裡的人。而且不只有年輕人是如此。似乎只剩下老年人，仍會與身邊的真實世界有所互動。何不讓你的眼睛休息一下，轉而跟身旁的人交談？

附言：若你正從行動裝置上讀取這則訊息，是可以被原諒的。

3-4 英文句子裡有「you」, 中文為什麼沒有翻呢?

可以翻出「你」,但翻了卻顯得多餘。 ▶

關鍵例句搶先看 ▶

The point is that through reading you gain knowledge and improve language skills in a way that addictive but basically pointless cellphone games never could.

重點是,閱讀能增長知識並提升語言能力。在某種程度上,玩手機遊戲永遠無法達到這種效果,只會讓人成癮,而且根本毫無意義。

基礎技巧提點

1 看完整個句子、段落、文章,依內容判定英文單字所代表的意思,在不同內容下,同一英文單字所表示的涵意,也許會有所不同。

2 表示書籍類型的英文用字,需查證固有譯名:「novel－長篇小説」、「autobiography－自傳」、「fiction－小説」、「non-fiction－散文」。

3 「in a way」,表示「就某種程度上」。

✏ **試著翻翻看** ▶ **試著翻畫底線的部分**

　　Teenagers should read more books. ❶ It doesn't matter what you read-novels, autobiographies, fiction or non-fiction. ❷ The point is that through reading, you gain knowledge and improve language skills in a way that addictive but basically pointless cellphone games never could. If you don't have much money, the library is happy to lend you some, and you can borrow as many as you like. When you can't sleep at night or you are feeling bored, turn on the light and open a good book.

❶ _____

_____

_____

❷ _____

_____

_____

❶ It doesn't matter what you read-novels, autobiographies, fiction or non-fiction.

各種類型的書籍都行－長篇小說、自傳、小說，亦或是寫實文學。

| 為什麼這樣翻 1 ┈┈┈┈┈┈┈┈┈┈┈┈┈┈┈┈┈┈┈┈┈┈┈┈┈┈┈

依前句「青少年應該多閱讀」，以及破折號（ ── ）後列出的四種文學體類型，可以知道「what you read」，指的是「書籍」，應適時加入譯出文，譯作「各種類型的書籍」。

在不同內容下，同一英文單字所表示的涵意也許會有所不同；「fiction」用於書籍分類時，即表示「小説類」，用於其他領域為「假象；虛構之事」的意思。

❷ The point is that through reading, you gain knowledge and improve language skills in a way that addictive but basically pointless cellphone games never could.

重點是，閱讀能增長知識並提升語言能力。就某種程度上，玩手機遊戲永遠無法達到這種效果，只會讓人成癮，而且根本毫無意義。

| 為什麼這樣翻 2 ⋯⋯⋯⋯⋯⋯⋯⋯⋯⋯⋯⋯⋯⋯⋯⋯⋯

　　全文以第二人稱「you」寫作，表示泛指所有閱讀這篇文章的讀者，不需特意將主詞「you」譯出。文章表達對讀者的呼籲之意明確，若再譯出主詞，會有贅字的問題。「...you gain knowledge and improve language skills...」，若將「你」譯出，「……你能增長知識、提升語言能力」，顯得有些多餘，譯文亦不夠順暢。

　　「in a way」有「就某種程度上」、「以另一個角度來看」、「就某種層面來看」的意思。

❶ It doesn't matter what you read-novels, autobiographies, fiction or non-fiction.

看什麼書都可以－長篇小說、自傳、小說，或者非小說。

| 為什麼還能這樣翻 1 ⋯⋯⋯⋯⋯⋯⋯⋯⋯⋯⋯⋯⋯⋯⋯⋯⋯⋯⋯

　　依前句「青少年應該多閱讀」，以及破折號（──）後列出的四種文學體類型，可以知道「what you read」，指的是「書籍」。「what you read」，亦可譯作「看什麼書都可以」。「non-fiction」，亦可譯作「非小說」。

❷ The point is that through reading, you gain knowledge and improve language skills in a way that addictive but basically pointless cellphone games never could.

重點是，閱讀有助增長知識、提升語言能力，就某種程度上，這些是使人成癮但基本上卻毫無意義的手機遊戲，永遠無法提供的益處。

| 為什麼還能這樣翻 2 ⋯⋯⋯⋯⋯⋯⋯⋯⋯⋯⋯⋯⋯⋯⋯⋯⋯⋯⋯⋯

　　「... through reading you gain knowledge and improve language skills...」，其語意肯定且正向，因此在譯文「閱讀

218

增長知識、提升語言能力」加上「有助」兩字譯作「閱讀有助增長知識、提升語言能力」，並在「...cellphone games never could」的譯文「永遠無法提供的」加上「益處」兩字譯作「永遠無法提供的益處」，使內容通順且相互呼應。

全文翻譯

青少年應該多閱讀。各種類型的書籍都行－長篇小說、自傳、小說，亦或是散文。重點是，閱讀能增長知識並提升語言能力。就某種程度上，玩手機遊戲永遠無法達到這種效果，只會讓人成癮，而且根本毫無意義。若你沒有太多錢可以拿來添購書籍，圖書館很樂意借你書，而且想借多少，就有多少。當你晚上睡不著，或是感到無聊時，你可以開盞燈，讀本好書。

看到「if」不能直接翻成「假如」嗎?

關鍵技巧 要先了解英文原句的上下文脈絡,跳脫「逐字翻譯」的生硬翻法。 ▶

關鍵例句搶先看 ▶

If you bet just £100 on them at the start of the season, you would have won half a million pounds!

要是你在球季開始便下注一百英鎊賭他們贏,就能抱回五十萬英鎊呢!

基礎技巧提點

1 依文章語意與情境背景,以最貼切的譯文敘述表達,必要時可在譯文後,以圓括弧加上註解,並適時加入譯出語。

2 各國貨幣符號儘量譯出固有譯名,但若是常用且辨識率高的貨幣,則只以符號譯出即可。

✏️ **試著翻翻看** ▶ 試著翻畫底線的部分

The little known team who were bottom of the league in 2015 and only narrowly avoided relegation that season have beaten their more famous rivals such as Manchester United, Liverpool and Chelsea to win the world's richest football league.

❶ In what has been called one of the greatest upsets in sporting history, the team with odds of 5000-1 against have done the impossible. That's worse odds than for the discovery of the Loch Ness Monster or Lady Gaga becoming US president in 2020. ❷ If you bet just £100 on them at the start of the season, you would have won half a million pounds! And people did, including Tom Hanks, who claimed he did just that.

❶ _____

_____

❷ _____

_____

❶ In what has been called one of the greatest upsets in sporting history, the team with odds of 5000-1 against have done the impossible.

它被稱為運動史上最爆冷門的結果之一。該隊賠率是投注一英鎊，獲利五千英鎊，而結果竟跌破眾人眼鏡。

| 為什麼這樣翻 1 ....

　　由接續的文章內容「… £100… won half a million pounds…」，可以判定為「固定賠率博彩」，符合「5000-1」的賠率，也就是投注一英鎊，就能獲利五千英鎊，而且本金也可拿回。

　　「have done the impossible」，字面上是「完成了不可能的任務」的意思，但譯作「跌破眾人眼鏡」，其語氣更能與前文的「爆冷門」相呼應。

❷ If you bet just £100 on them at the start of the season, you would have won half a million pounds!

要是你在球季開始便下注一百英鎊賭他們贏，就能抱回五十萬英鎊呢！

| 為什麼這樣翻 2 ⋯⋯⋯⋯⋯⋯⋯⋯⋯⋯⋯⋯⋯⋯⋯⋯⋯⋯

　　英文表示金額的譯文，不需再換算幣值，採直譯方式。譯出文是以金額加上該國貨幣名稱的方式表示。「… bet just £100…」，用於博彩的投注方式，有其特定術語，故需譯作「**下注**一百英鎊」，而不是「**賭**一百英鎊」。「… won half a million pounds…」，以「抱回」取代「贏得」，更能突顯其語帶興奮的語氣。

❶ In what has been called one of the greatest upsets in sporting history, the team with odds of 5000-1 against have done the impossible.

這個結果跌破眾人眼鏡，被稱為運動史上最爆冷門的結果之一；該隊賠率是投注 £1，獲利 £5,000。

| 為什麼還能這樣翻 1 ⋯⋯⋯⋯⋯⋯⋯⋯⋯⋯⋯⋯⋯⋯⋯⋯⋯⋯⋯⋯⋯⋯⋯⋯

　　各國貨幣符號儘量譯出固有譯名，但若是常用且辨識率高的貨幣，則只以符號譯出即可。「一英鎊」、「五千英鎊」亦可譯作符號加阿拉伯數字的組合：「£1」、「£5,000」。

❷ If you bet just £100 on them at the start of the season, you would have won half a million pounds!

要是你在球季開始便下注 1 百英鎊押他們贏，就能抱回 50 萬英鎊呢！

| 為什麼還能這樣翻 2 ⋯⋯⋯⋯⋯⋯⋯⋯⋯⋯⋯⋯⋯⋯⋯⋯⋯⋯⋯⋯⋯⋯⋯⋯

　　表示金額的數值，以中文字或阿拉伯數字譯出皆可。百位數（含）以上的數值，可混合使用阿拉伯數字與單位量詞

的方式表示。「£100」、「half a million pounds」，亦可譯作阿拉伯數字與量詞單位的組合：「1 百英鎊」、「50 萬英鎊」。「賭他們贏」，亦可譯作「押他們贏」。「if」譯作「假如」、「要是」，語氣皆屬假設口吻。

全文翻譯

　　這支沒沒無名的隊伍，二〇一五年在聯盟的排名不但墊底，當季還險些被降組，如今卻打敗了名氣比他們大的對手：曼聯（Manchester United）、利物浦隊（Liverpool）、切爾西隊（Chelsea），在全球最富有的足球聯盟中，勇奪冠軍。

　　它被稱為運動史上最爆冷門的結果之一。該隊賠率是投注一英鎊，獲利五千英鎊，而結果竟跌破眾人眼鏡。是比找到尼斯湖水怪，或是女神卡卡在二〇二〇年成為美國總統的賠率高得多（賠率愈高，表示實際發生的機率愈低）。要是你在球季開始便下注一百英鎊賭他們贏，就能抱回五十萬英鎊呢！的確有人這麼做，包括名演員湯姆·漢克斯（Tom Hanks），他宣稱自己正是如此。

關鍵 技巧 除了了解英文原句的上下文脈絡，更要試著揣摩中文才會有的自然語氣，你才能斷絕「中式英文」！ ▶

關鍵例句搶先看 ●

For as little as US$150, you can have your genome mapped providing you with a detailed insight into which diseases you are likely to contract.

只要一百五十美金，就能擁有個人的基因圖譜，其精闢的細節，能讓你瞭解可能承襲的疾病。

基礎技巧提點

1 各國貨幣符號盡量譯出譯名，若是常用且辨識率高的貨幣，可只以符號譯出。如美國貨幣「美金」的符號「US$」，在國際間屬辨識率極高的符號。

2 「saliva」的俗名是「口水」，學名稱作「唾液」。通常在翻譯時，會以學名譯出，但學名的常見普遍性若低於其俗名，則需以圓括弧加註俗名或原文。

試著翻翻看 ▶ 試著翻畫底線的部分

Would you want to know when you are going to die?

❶ Advances in medical technology mean that it might not be as far off as you might think. ❷ For as little as US$150, you can have your genome mapped providing you with a detailed insight into which diseases you are likely to contract.

You simply send a sample of your saliva off in the post, and a few weeks later, you know whether you are likely to die of cancer or heart disease. The idea is that you then don't have to actually die. You visit the doctor and get treatment before you get sick.

❶ _____

_____

_____

❷ _____

_____

❶ Advances in medical technology mean that it might not be as far off as you might think.

隨著醫療科技的進步，意味著這也許沒有想像中的遙不可及。

| 為什麼這樣翻 1 ‥‥‥‥‥‥‥‥‥‥‥‥‥‥‥‥‥‥‥‥‥‥

　　適時加入譯出文「隨著」，作為起頭的導語，使本句譯文更通順。「mean that」有「代表；表示；意味」的意思。「far off」是「距離遙遠」的意思，依本句語意，以中文成語「遙不可及」譯出最為貼切，用以形容對某件事的想像或看法。

❷ For as little as US$150, you can have your genome mapped providing you with a detailed insight into which diseases you are likely to contract.

只要一百五十美金，就能擁有個人的基因圖譜，其精闢的細節，能讓你瞭解可能承襲的疾病。

| 為什麼這樣翻 2 ⋯⋯⋯⋯⋯⋯⋯⋯⋯⋯⋯⋯⋯⋯⋯

　　各國貨幣符號盡量譯出譯名，避免誤解的情況發生；「US$」是「美金」。

　　「you can have your genome mapped」，若逐字直譯成「你就能要人製作你的基因圖譜」，會使得譯文不夠通順，故應在不更改原意的情況下，將譯文以符合中文語法及原文語意的方式，譯作「就能擁有個人的基因圖譜」。

　　「contract」在這裡譯作「承襲」，以符合用人體內定不可違的「基因」，所剖析的可能患有疾病。

❶ Advances in medical technology mean that it might not be as far off as you might think.

隨著醫療科技的進步，代表這也許沒有想像中的那麼遙不可及。

| 為什麼還能這樣翻 1 ···

「意味著這也許沒有想像中的遙不可及」，亦可將「意味著」改寫作「表示」、「代表」。**在譯出文加入「那麼」兩字，修飾「遙不可及」，表示突顯與強調的語氣，不影響原意。**

❷ For as little as US$150, you can have your genome mapped providing you with a detailed insight into which diseases you are likely to contract.

只要 USD$150，就能擁有專屬的基因圖譜，其精闢的細節，能讓你瞭解自己可能承襲的疾病。

| 為什麼還能這樣翻 2 ···

美國貨幣「美金」的符號「US$」，在國際間屬辨識率極高的符號，故「一百五十美金」亦可譯作「USD$150」。

「就能擁有個人的基因圖譜」，亦可譯作「就能擁有專屬的基因圖譜」。「for」作介系詞用，在本文中是「換取（某物）」的意思；譯文譯作「只要」，用於突顯以某種價格換取某物的交易，屬於很划算的狀態。

全文翻譯

想知道自己什麼時候會死亡嗎？

隨著醫療科技的進步，意味著這也許沒有想像中的遙不可及。只要一百五十美金，就能擁有個人的基因圖譜，其精闢的細節，能讓你瞭解可能承襲的疾病。

只需郵寄唾液樣本，然後幾星期後，就能知道自己是否可能死於癌症，或是心臟病發。用意是讓你可不必因這些病因死亡；在患病前先找醫師提供治療。

correspond 為什麼會翻成「不謀而合」?

關鍵技巧 為了能有更好的中文譯文,多學潤飾語句的詞藻能讓譯文更加自然、通順! ▶

關鍵例句搶先看 ▶

The location of twenty-two known Mayan cities corresponded with the star charts, but there was a 23rd location but no known city.

已知的二十二個馬雅古城,與馬雅星座圖對應的位置,不謀而合;可是還有第二十三個相對應位置,卻尚未出現已知的古城。

基礎技巧提點

1 「Canadian Space Agency」,是「加拿大太空總署」。

2 英文常以代名詞代替接續敘述中的名詞主詞,譯文需在主詞不夠明確的情況下,譯出完整的名詞主詞。

✒ 試著翻翻看 ▶ **試著翻畫底線的部分**

Recently a fifteen-year-old Canadian boy outsmarted the experts and discovered an ancient Mayan city. ❶ He has named the city hidden deep in the Mexican jungle 'Mouth of Fire'. William, from Quebec, has been fascinated by the ancient Mayan since his interest was sparked by the reporting of the end of the Mayan calendar in 2012. William made the discovery by overlaying ancient Mayan star charts onto Google maps. ❷ The location of twenty-two known Mayan cities corresponded with the star charts, but there was a 23rd location but no known city.

❶ _____

_____

_____

_____

❷ _____

_____

_____

_____

✒ 你翻對了嗎？

❶ He has named the city hidden deep in the Mexican jungle 'Mouth of Fire'.

並將這座深藏於墨西哥叢林的城市命名為－「火之口」（Mouth of Fire）。

| 為什麼這樣翻 1 ⋯⋯⋯⋯⋯⋯⋯⋯⋯⋯⋯⋯⋯⋯⋯⋯⋯⋯⋯⋯⋯⋯⋯⋯

　　本段尚未提及這位十五歲青少年的名字，因而此句譯文不適合直接將他的名字譯出。

　　原文於句中大寫即表示為專有名詞，需查證固有譯名，並以圓括弧引註原文。以破折號介紹某種說法，也有強調語氣、定義的用意。

❷ The location of twenty-two known Mayan cities corresponded with the star charts, but there was a 23rd location but no known city.

已知的二十二個馬雅古城,與馬雅星座圖對應的位置,不謀而合;可是還有第二十三個相對應位置,卻尚未出現已知的古城。

| 為什麼這樣翻 2 ⋯⋯⋯⋯⋯⋯⋯⋯⋯⋯⋯⋯⋯⋯⋯⋯⋯⋯⋯⋯⋯⋯⋯⋯

「... Mayan cities corresponded with the star charts...」,以「不謀而合」形容相對應位置之間的符合程度,使得語氣更增添了一絲令人感到神祕驚訝,甚至肯定的情緒,替接下來的「but...」敘述,埋下一種令人期待的發展。

「but there was a 23rd location but no known city.」,以「可是還有」的譯文來表示「第二十三個相對應位置尚未出現已知的古城」,呼應本文所表達的神祕驚奇氛圍。

❶ He has named the city hidden deep in the Mexican jungle 'Mouth of Fire'.

他將這座深藏墨西哥叢林的城市，取名為「火之口」（Mouth of Fire）。

| 為什麼還能這樣翻 1 ···

　　本句主詞亦可以代名詞「他」表示，但仍不適合以人名表示；其名字只在下一段出現，因此前兩段屬導言性質。也可以用逗號區隔句子中不同的元素或概念，譯作「……城市，取名為「火之口」（Mouth of Fire）」。

❷ The location of twenty-two known Mayan cities corresponded with the star charts, but there was a 23rd location but no known city.

22 個已知的馬雅古城，與馬雅星座圖的位置相互對應；但是第 23 個地點，卻尚未出現已知的對應古城。

| 為什麼還能這樣翻 2 ···

　　「已知的二十二個馬雅古城」，亦可譯作「22 個已知的馬雅古城」。「與馬雅星座圖對應的位置，不謀而合」，

亦可譯作「與馬雅星座圖的位置相互對應」，但較無引出古文明的神祕感氛圍。「可是還有第二十三個相對應位置，卻尚未出現已知的古城」，亦可將「location」譯作「地點」；在「已知古城」加入「對應」譯文，符合文章的整體性。

全文翻譯

　　最近有位十五歲的加拿大青少年，勝過專家，發現了一座馬雅古城，並將這座深藏於墨西哥叢林的城市命名為－「火之口」（Mouth of Fire）。威廉來自加拿大魁北克省（Quebec），著迷於古老的馬雅文化。馬雅曆法只算到二〇一二年所引發的大肆報導，引起他對該文化的興趣。他將古老的馬雅星座圖，與Google 提供的衛星影像相互對應，發現了這座古城。已知的二十二個馬雅古城，與馬雅星座圖對應的位置，不謀而合；可是還有第二十三個相對應位置，卻尚未出現已知的古城。

原句沒有「but」，那為什麼譯文有「但」的翻譯呢？

關鍵技巧 避免「逐字翻譯」的技巧 ▶

關鍵例句搶先看 ●

The translator, whose only language was English, noticed a lack of Korean-English translators in the UK, so she started to teach herself the language.

該書譯者只會一種語言－英文，但她發現英國缺乏韓文譯英文的譯者，於是便開始自學韓文。

基礎技巧提點

1 驚嘆號「！」，用於表達驚訝的情緒。

2 譯文以白話文為主，以正常速度唸文章時，該停頓換氣時，原則上就是需要下逗號的位置，譯文不需配合原文語法的標點符號使用。

3 英文片語、慣用語的意思，需依其涵意，以最貼切的中文譯出，不可逐字直譯。

試著翻翻看 ▶ 試著翻畫底線的部分

An international book prize has been won by a Korean book.

❶ Nothing out of the ordinary there you may think until you realize that it was translated into English by a translator who until 2010 couldn't speak a word of Korean. ❷ The translator, whose only language was English, noticed a lack of Korean-English translators in the UK, so she started to teach herself the language.

Her translation of the book about a woman who "wants to reject human brutality" was described by the judging panel as "unforgettably powerful and original". Both the author and translator will share the £50,000 prize.

❶ _____

_____

❷ _____

_____

❶ Nothing out of the ordinary there you may think until you realize that it was translated into English by a translator who until 2010 couldn't speak a word of Korean.

這並不讓人覺得有什麼稀奇，直到發現獲獎的是翻譯文學書籍；特別的是，這本韓文書籍的譯者，自二〇一〇年才開始學習韓文。

| 為什麼這樣翻 1 ....

「nothing out of the ordinary」，是「沒有什麼特別；稀鬆平常；平平常常」的意思，是貶義的語意，在譯文加上「特別的是」，與「這並不讓人覺得有什麼稀奇」做出對比且相呼應，使譯文句子結構更完整。分號「；」，用於連獨立的句子，比起句號更能顯示出兩個句子之間的相關性。

❷ The translator, whose only language was English, noticed a lack of Korean-English translators in the UK, so she started to teach herself the language.

該書譯者只會一種語言－英文，但她發現英國缺乏韓文譯英文的譯者，於是便開始自學韓文。

| 為什麼這樣翻 2 ┈┈┈┈┈┈┈┈┈┈┈┈┈┈┈┈┈┈┈┈┈┈┈┈┈┈┈┈┈

　　破折號「 ─ 」，用於介紹某種說法，加入強調語氣。「noticed a lack of Korean-English translators in the UK」不可逐字直譯成「發現缺乏韓文譯英文的譯者在英國」，中文語法習慣先表明主詞、時間、地點，以符合中文語法。

　　以代名詞「她」，表示「該書譯者」，不在同段落句子中，重覆譯出名詞主詞。

　　中文譯文加入原文沒有出現的「但」，與下一句的譯文「於是」相呼應，能使譯文更加順暢，且不影響原意。

❶ Nothing out of the ordinary there you may think until you realize that it was translated into English by a translator who until 2010 couldn't speak a word of Korean.

乍聽之下，你會認為這是很平常的事，但是當你知道獲獎的是翻譯文學書籍，而且該書譯者是在 2010 年才開始學習韓文之後，便不會這麼覺得了。

| 為什麼還能這樣翻 1 ·····

　　在不影響語意清況下，本句譯文開頭加上「乍聽之下」，導出實際結果將與接下來敘述相反的語意；亦在句尾加入譯文「便不會這麼覺得了」，使句子更具完整性，與句首的敘述相呼應。「二〇一〇年」亦可以阿拉伯數字譯作「2010 年」，唯全文需統一譯法。

❷ The translator, whose only language was English, noticed a lack of Korean-English translators in the UK, so she started to teach herself the language.

該書譯者只會英文一種語言。她注意到英國缺乏韓譯英的譯者，也因此開始自學韓文。

┃為什麼還能這樣翻 2

　　「該書譯者只會一種語言－英文」，亦可譯作「該書譯者只會英文一種語言」，並以句號結束。「韓文譯英文」，中文口語常以譯出語和譯入語的第一個字，簡稱為「韓譯英」。

全文翻譯

　　韓文書籍贏得國際書獎！

　　這並不讓人覺得有什麼稀奇，直到發現獲獎的是翻譯文學書籍；特別的是，這本韓文書籍的譯者，自二〇一〇年才開始學習韓文。該書譯者只會一種語言－英文，但她發現英國缺乏韓文譯英文的譯者，於是便開始自學韓文。

　　她翻譯的這本書籍，是講述一位女性「想除去人性的殘酷」，評審專家形容它「令人難忘、震撼，具獨到的原創性」。作者與譯者共同獲得£50,000 的獎金。

「Spokesman」不能只翻成「發言人」嗎？

關鍵技巧 當然可以，但也要細看上下文，若是指「總統發言人」，那麼翻成「白宮發言人」更準確！ ▶

關鍵例句搶先看 ●

A spokesman said that the president drank the filtered water to "show it was safe".

白宮發言人表示，總統喝下過濾後的飲用水，是為了向大家「證明水質安全」。

基礎技巧提點

1 若為特定人士的頭銜，需適時加上該國家或組織名稱，讓譯文更加清晰。

2 人名、地名、組織名、職稱與頭銜，需查證是否已約定成俗的特定譯名。

3 人名、地名、組織名，若是十分普遍且常見的譯名，可不需再加註原文，但為求慎重起見，通常會在第一次出現於譯文中時，以圓括弧引註原文。

✐ 試著翻翻看▶ 試著翻畫底線的部分

President Obama drinks water in crisis-hit town

❶ President Obama took a sip of water in the town of Flint, Michigan. The gesture, in response to a letter from an eight-year-old girl, is being seen as an attempt to reassure its 100,000 residents.

For over a year the people of Flint have been slowly poisoned by lead in their water supply. The scandal erupted after the town controversially changed its water supply. President Obama declared a state of emergency in January and ordered federal aid for the crisis. Residents have since been provided with free faucet filters. ❷ A spokesman said that the president drank the filtered water to "show it was safe".

❶ _____

_____

❷ _____

_____

❶ President Obama took a sip of water in the town of Flint, Michigan. The gesture, in response to a letter from an eight-year-old girl,...

美國總統歐巴馬（Obama），喝了一口密西根州弗林特鎮（Flint, Michigan）的飲用水。歐巴馬總統以這個舉動，回應一位八歲女童的陳情信，⋯。

| 為什麼這樣翻 1 ⋯⋯⋯⋯⋯⋯⋯⋯⋯⋯⋯⋯⋯⋯⋯⋯⋯⋯⋯⋯⋯⋯

　　若為特定人士的頭銜，應適時加上國家名稱；「Obama」為美國現任總統，固在譯文補充說明為「美國總統歐巴馬（Obama）」。**英文敘述地方時，會以規模劃分的程度，由小到大敘述：「the town of Flint, Michigan」，中文譯文則是相反，是由規模大到小的形式才符合中文語法。**「a letter」，依文意譯作「陳情信」，較單純譯作「信」，來得更切合主題。

❷ A spokesman said that the president drank the filtered water to "show it was safe".

白宮發言人表示，總統喝下過濾後的飲用水，是為了向大家「證明水質安全」。

| 為什麼這樣翻 2 ⋯⋯⋯⋯⋯⋯⋯⋯⋯⋯⋯⋯⋯⋯⋯⋯⋯⋯⋯⋯

原文僅以「a spokesman said that...」來發表以下談話，若只譯作「發言人」，會有種讓人不知所言為何的感覺，因此參照上下文，並以本句「the president drank the filtered water to "show it was safe"」足以得知，是替總統發言的人，在美國，替總統發言的人即白宮發言人，故譯文需補充加上「白宮」兩字。

🖋 也可以這麼翻

❶ President Obama took a sip of water in the town of Flint, Michigan. The gesture, in response to a letter from an eight-year-old girl,...

美國總統歐巴馬（Obama），喝下密西根州弗林特鎮（Flint, Michigan）的飲用水。他以這個舉動，回應一封八歲女童寫的陳情信，……。

| 為什麼還能這樣翻 1 ·······································

「took a sip of water」，亦可譯作「喝下」，不用必須著墨在「喝一口」的原文直譯，並不影響原意，其重點是「喝」，不在於喝了多少。「in response ...」，**因為接續敘述前文，故可直接將主詞以代名詞主詞「他」，譯作「他以這個舉動……」**，仍可清楚知道，做這個舉動是歐巴馬為了達成特定目標的用意。

❷ A spokesman said that the president drank the filtered water to "show it was safe".

白宮發言人表示：「總統喝下過濾後的飲用水，是為了向大家證明水質安全無虞。」

「A spokesman said that...」，亦可直接將譯文譯作白宮發言人所發表的話，以冒號加引號「：「」」，將其敘述的發言內容，涵蓋在引號中。

全文翻譯

歐巴馬總統喝下陷入飲用水安全風暴的鎮上飲用水

美國總統歐巴馬（Obama），喝了一口密西根州弗林特鎮（Flint, Michigan）的飲用水。歐巴馬總統以這個舉動，回應一位八歲女童的陳情信，此舉更被視為是試圖向弗林特鎮的十萬名居民，做出飲用水安全無虞的保證。

一年多來，弗林特鎮飲用水水源中的鉛，慢慢地毒害了當地居民。這件醜聞是在該鎮引發爭議性地更換供水水源後，才爆發了出來。一月，歐巴馬總統宣佈該州進入緊急狀態，並下令聯邦政府協助處理此危機。居民也開始收到政府提供的免費水龍頭濾水器。白宮發言人表示，總統喝下過濾後的飲用水，是為了向大家「證明水質安全」。

每次看到「英文數字」就不知道怎麼翻嗎？

關鍵技巧 細看上下文並用中文思維，翻譯數字也不是問題！ ▶

關鍵例句搶先看 ◉

So far this year 330 wildfires have been reported, more than double the annual average.

今年至目前為止，獲報的森林野火案件已有 **330** 起，是年度平均案件次數多出一倍以上。

基礎技巧提點

1 留意英文語法中的時態與被動語態，譯文需符合中文語法。

2 「double」，即「兩倍；多一倍」。要小心別誤譯成「多兩倍」，也就是「三倍」的意思。

3 表示溫度的數值與溫度單位符號，譯文能以阿拉伯數字與符號表示，或是完全以中文字的方式譯出。

🖊 **試著翻翻看** ▶ 試著翻畫底線的部分

The entire sixty thousand population of Fort McMurray, Alberta has been forced to evacuate as a wildfire jumps a river and threatens the city.

❶ <u>So far this year 330 wildfires have been reported, more than double the annual average.</u> This year's fires have been described as a perfect storm of high temperatures, dry conditions, global warming and El Niño. ❷ <u>Temperatures in Fort McMurray have soared to 32°C, which is significantly higher than the usual May high of around 14°C.</u> Scientists have described the current El Niño event as one of the strongest on record with drought in Africa and a reduced monsoon in India.

❶ _____

_____

_____

❷ _____

_____

❶ So far this year 330 wildfires have been reported, more than double the annual average.

今年至目前為止，獲報的森林野火案件共計三百三十起，比年度平均案件次數多出一倍以上。

| 為什麼這樣翻 1 ⋯⋯⋯⋯⋯⋯⋯⋯⋯⋯⋯⋯⋯⋯⋯⋯⋯⋯⋯⋯⋯⋯⋯⋯

「have been reported」是現在完成式被動語態，若將譯文直譯成「已經被報告」，並不符合中文語法。

「double」是「兩倍；雙倍；多一倍」的意思。將表示數量、數值的原文，轉換成另一種語言時，絕對不能有誤，將完全影響譯文的正確性。例如：四的兩倍為八；四的多一倍為八，但是若譯成四的多兩倍，其結果則為十二。

❷ Temperatures in Fort McMurray have soared to 32°C, which is significantly higher than the usual May high of around 14°C.

麥克默里堡的氣溫驟升至攝氏三十二度，比平常五月最高溫攝氏十四度左右，高出許多。

| 為什麼這樣翻 2 ⋯⋯⋯⋯⋯⋯⋯⋯⋯⋯⋯⋯⋯⋯⋯⋯⋯

　　第二次出現在譯文中的城市名，直接以譯名表示即可。動詞「soar」，用在溫度變化時，譯文應以「驟升」，而不能以「高漲」或「增強」來表示。譯文需符合中文語法，將句中所提及的地點、時間，置於句子的開頭，再接續敘述。「around＋數值」，意即「大約；左右；上下；差不多」的意思。

❶ So far this year 330 wildfires have been reported, more than double the annual average.

今年至目前為止,獲報的森林野火案件已有 330 起,是年度平均案件次數的二倍以上。

| 為什麼還能這樣翻 1 ⋯⋯⋯⋯⋯⋯⋯⋯⋯⋯⋯⋯⋯⋯⋯⋯⋯⋯⋯⋯⋯

「330 wildfires have been reported」,不可直譯作「已經有」三百三十起森林野火被通報」,本文以是第三者的角度寫作,因此譯文除符合中文語法之外,譯文亦需以報導性質慣用字呈現,因此譯作「獲報的森林野火案件已有 330 起」。「比⋯⋯多出一倍以上」,亦可譯作「是⋯⋯的二倍以上」。

❷ Temperatures in Fort McMurray have soared to 32°C, which is significantly higher than the usual May high of around 14°C.

麥克默里堡的氣溫急升至 32°C,比平常五月最高溫約 14°C,還要高出許多。

| 為什麼還能這樣翻 2 ⋯⋯⋯⋯⋯⋯

　　表達溫度急速變化時，譯文應以「驟升」、「急升」，而來表示。「攝氏三十二度」，亦可以阿拉伯數字配合溫度單位符號，譯作「32°C」。「攝氏十四度左右」，亦可以阿拉伯數字配合溫度單位符號，並以相同語意的不同說法，譯作「約 14°C」。

全文翻譯

　　加拿大亞伯達省麥克默里堡（McMurray, Alberta），全市六萬居民被迫撤離，因為森林野火躍過河川，威脅了全市的安全。

　　今年至目前為止，獲報的森林野火案件共計三百三十起，比年度平均案件次數多出一倍以上。今年的森林野火，被形容成在高溫、乾燥、全球暖化，以及聖嬰現象（El Niño）下的大爆發。麥克默里堡的氣溫驟升至攝氏三十二度，比平常五月最高溫攝氏十四度左右，高出許多。科學家將目前聖嬰現象情況，形容為有記錄以來，威力最強的其中一次，包括造成非洲乾旱，以及印度雨季的縮短。

「日期」、「時間」的翻譯為什麼不能直接照英文原句的順序翻呢？

關鍵技巧 中文和英文的語序不同，日期、時間的表達方式當然也不同！ ▶

關鍵例句搶先看 ●

In order to comply with health and safety regulations a fire drill will be held on Wednesday, August 5th at 11:15am.

謹定於八月五日，星期三上午十一時十五分，依健康與安全法規之規定，進行消防演習。

基礎技巧提點

1. 公文性質，或正式文件的內容，時間、日期皆需以全中文字譯出。

2. 傳達特定訊息或要求的文章，應以明快俐落的譯文詮釋。

3. 英文有被動語態，但若主詞為事／物時，中文譯文則不譯出「被」來突顯其意涵。

✏ 試著翻翻看▶ 試著翻畫底線的部分

To: All employees

Subject: Fire drill

❶ In order to comply with health and safety regulations a fire drill will be held on Wednesday, August 5th at 11:15am. Upon hearing the alarm, everyone inside the building must promptly leave the building in an orderly manner from the nearest exit and assemble in one of the three designated evacuation points. ❷ The location of your nearest evacuation point is displayed in every office and corridor. Management understands that this may cause some inconvenience; however, your cooperation in this matter is appreciated.

❶ _____

_____

_____

❷ _____

_____

❶ In order to comply with health and safety regulations a fire drill will be held on Wednesday, August 5th at 11:15am.

謹定於八月五日，星期三上午十一時十五分，依健康與安全法規之規定，進行消防演習。

| 為什麼這樣翻 1 ⋯⋯⋯⋯⋯⋯⋯⋯⋯⋯⋯⋯⋯⋯⋯⋯⋯⋯⋯⋯⋯⋯⋯⋯⋯⋯⋯⋯

　　英文縮寫「am」、「pm」，在譯文中需以中文字表示。「11:15am」，表示「上午十一時十五分」。

　　「a fire drill will be held」，**不可逐字以英文被動語態直譯作「消防演習會被舉行」，不符合中文語法**。中文語序會將日期、時間，寫在事件之前。**本文為公文文件性質，固將內容中特定的日期與時間，加以「謹定於」譯出文表示。**

❷ The location of your nearest evacuation point is displayed in every office and corridor.

辦公室和走廊,皆有陳列距離你最近的疏散點位置圖。

| 為什麼這樣翻 2 ⋯⋯⋯⋯

　　英文有被動語態,但若主詞為事／物時,中文譯文則不譯出「被」來突顯其意涵。「The location of your nearest evacuation point is displayed...」,是英文的被動語態,但其主詞為「The location of your nearest evacuation point」,故不應將「被」譯出,以符合中文語法。

❶ In order to comply with health and safety regulations a fire drill will be held on Wednesday, August 5th at 11:15am.

謹定於 8 月 5 日星期三，上午 11 時 15 分，依健康與安全法規之規定，進行消防演習。

| 為什麼還能這樣翻 1 ···

　　「八月五日」，亦可譯作「8 月 5 日」。「Wednesday」是有特定單字的字詞，並非以數字計算，因此譯文不可將中文譯作「星期三」的數值，轉換成阿拉伯數字。「上午十一時十五分」，亦可譯作「上午 11 時（點）15 分」，或以阿拉伯數字搭配冒號「：」的方式譯出，譯作「11:35」。「in order to（做某事）」，譯作「符合」、「依……規定」。

❷ The location of your nearest evacuation point is displayed in every office and corridor.

距你最近的疏散點位置圖，皆陳列於各辦公室和走廊。

| 為什麼還能這樣翻 2

先譯出地點的譯法：「辦公室和走廊，皆有陳列距離你最近的疏散點位置圖」，若改寫作「距你最近的疏散點位置圖，皆陳列於各辦公室和走廊。」亦十分通暢，且不影響原意。

全文翻譯

致：全體員工

主題：消防演習

謹定於八月五日，星期三上午十一時十五分，依健康與安全法規之規定，進行消防演習。警鈴響起時，所有在室內的人員，必須立即有秩序地從最近的緊急出口離開建築物，並在三個指定疏散點的其中一處集合。辦公室和走廊，皆有陳列距離你最近的疏散點位置圖。公司了解這也許會造成些許不便，我們十分感激你對這次消防演習的配合。

「silently」翻成「安靜地」不就好了嗎？

文學翻譯小技巧：你的詞藻需要更精準！ ▶

關鍵例句搶先看 ▶

There it was standing silently with two dark menacing eyes looking right at him. Jason froze.

它就在那！死寂地站著，幽暗陰森的雙眸直盯著他。傑森嚇呆了，全身僵住。

基礎技巧提點

1. 小說體材的譯文用字，**需配合內容的情緒、背景設定、情境，以足以體現意境與節奏的譯出文**，加以修飾。

2. 小說體材文章，譯文只以音譯表示內容裡的角色人名譯文，不需再以圓括弧附註原文。

3. 本文內容充滿緊張懸疑氣氛，故譯文用字應選擇較貼近此風格的敘述方式。

4. 不逐字譯，要先看完整個句子、段落，再下筆，譯意不譯字。

✎ 試著翻翻看▶ 試著翻畫底線的部分

❶ Jason fumbled frantically with the door handle. Finally open, he burst out into the bright sunlight-his heart racing. Had he been seen? There was no way to know. Was it following him? His heart felt like it might explode in his chest as he thought about what he had just seen.

Feeling slightly better, he took a few steps and turned around the corner of the house, ❷ and there it was standing silently with two dark menacing eyes looking right at him. Jason froze. It took a step towards him and...

❶ _____

_____

_____

❷ _____

_____

_____

❶ Jason fumbled frantically with the door handle. Finally open, he burst out into the bright sunlight-his heart racing.

傑森狂亂地扭動著門把。門終於開啟，他突然置身耀眼的陽光下，心臟狂跳不已。

| 為什麼這樣翻 1 ....

　　破折號「 ── 」，用於強調語氣，也用於隔開兩個句子，與逗號「，」的作用雷同。

　　在「his heart racing」前，以中文逗號取代破折號表示，更能顯現出本段內容的緊湊、高度緊繃情境。整段敘述中發生的連續事件，中譯文若以破折號強調「his heart racing」，將較無法呈現其緊湊感。

❷ and there it was standing silently with two dark menacing eyes looking right at him. Jason froze.

它就在那！死寂地站著，幽暗陰森的雙眸直盯著他。傑森嚇呆了，全身僵住。

| 為什麼這樣翻 2 ⋯⋯⋯⋯⋯⋯⋯⋯⋯

驚嘆號「！」，用於表達突然間的驚訝。

「and there it was」，譯文以驚嘆號表示「它就在那」的語氣，會比使用中文逗號的接續敘述方式，更具震憾力，與前文「稍稍平復後⋯⋯」的情節氣氛形成對比，再次將讀者帶入緊張、懸疑的故事情節中。「silently」、「two dark menacing eyes」，以「死寂地」、「幽暗陰森的雙眸」，營造出令人恐懼的形象。

❶ Jason fumbled frantically with the door handle. Finally open, he burst out into the bright sunlight – his heart racing.

傑森發狂似地轉動門把。門終於開啟,他的心跳加速,眼前耀眼的陽光讓他不禁瞇起雙眼。

| 為什麼還能這樣翻 1 ………………………………………………………

「he burst out into the bright sunlight」,亦可加入譯出文「讓他不禁瞇起雙眼」,從黑暗處突然置身於亮處時,眼睛會因不適應,自然地瞇起,並不會更改原意。

❷ and there it was standing silently with two dark menacing eyes looking right at him. Jason froze.

它就在那!死寂地站著,幽暗陰森的雙眼直盯著他。驚嚇過度的傑森就佇在原地,動也不動。

| 為什麼還能這樣翻 2 ………………………………………………………

「雙眸」亦可譯作「雙眼」、「一雙眼睛」。「Jason froze」,形容傑森受到極度驚嚇,使得全身動彈不得且維持在原本姿勢。亦可譯作「驚嚇過度的傑森就佇在原地,動

也不動」；其「佇在原地」已表達傑森受驚嚇過度而造成他站著不動的意境，再補上「動也不動」，就又更強調了他受驚嚇的程度。

全文翻譯

　　傑森狂亂地扭動著門把。門終於開啟，他突然置身耀眼的陽光下，心臟狂跳不已。有被看見嗎？這點無從得知。有跟著他嗎？他一回想起剛才目睹的景象，就感覺心臟快要從胸口迸出。

　　稍稍平復後，他走了幾步，來到房屋的轉角處。它就在那！死寂地站著，幽暗陰森的雙眸直盯著他。傑森嚇呆了，全身僵住。它向前逼近一步，接著…

「使用說明」該怎麼翻？

關鍵技巧 掌握「簡明」、「扼要」原則 ▶

關鍵例句搶先看 ◉

Remove all inner packaging before use.

使用前先移除所有內包裝。

基礎技巧提點

1 英文句子中，若突然字母全以大寫方式表達時，表示強調。**在中文譯文中，一般以粗體字表示。有時亦會以放大的字體、套以不同顏色，或加上底線，以表示其強調之意。**

2 條列式內容，若項目標記為阿拉伯數字時，譯文應以中文字搭配頓號「、」或間隔號「‧」表示。

3 表示電流伏特的單位符號，因屬十分普遍常見且全球通用的符號，譯文可將該單位「v」直接以符號表示。

4 英文條列式內容的句子，以命令句方式表示，譯文需省略第二人稱主詞「you」。

✏ **試著翻翻看▸** **試著翻畫底線的部分**

Instructions for the correct usage of the microwave oven

1 Read these instructions carefully before attempting to operate this appliance.

2 Remove all outer packaging.

3 Place on a large flat surface with space for ventilation on all sides.

4 ❶ Remove all inner packaging before use.

5 Connect directly to a 110V wall outlet.

6 ❷ DO NOT cover the ventilation grill on the top of the oven.

7 Do NOT open the door while the oven is in operation.

❶ _____

_____

_____

❷ _____

_____

❶ Remove all inner packaging before use.

使用前先移除所有內包裝。

| 為什麼這樣翻 1 ⋯⋯⋯⋯⋯⋯⋯⋯⋯⋯⋯⋯⋯⋯⋯⋯⋯⋯⋯⋯⋯⋯

「before」是用於表示時間的引導詞，指「某個時間點之前」。譯文需符合中文語法，先譯出時間。並在譯文加入「先」，與「」（中文引號）有呼應效果，更為明確傳達指令。

❷ DO NOT cover the ventilation grill on the top of the oven.

請勿覆蓋機身上方的通風架。

| 為什麼這樣翻 2 ⋯⋯⋯⋯⋯⋯⋯⋯⋯⋯⋯⋯⋯⋯⋯⋯⋯⋯⋯⋯⋯⋯⋯⋯⋯⋯

　　英文句子中，若突然全以「大寫方式」表達時，表示強調。在中文譯文中，一般會以粗體字表示。「the oven」指的是微波爐，而微波爐是一台機器，由於本操作說明即是說明微波爐的使用方法，故譯作「機身」，而不譯作「微波爐」，這樣的譯法讓文字簡潔，更符合說明書指明重點的用意。

❶ Remove all inner packaging before use.

請於使用前移除所有內包裝。

| 為什麼還能這樣翻 1 ···

　　屬於使用說明性質的命令句敘述句中，加入譯出文「請」，但省略主詞「you」。不影響原意。

❷ DO NOT cover the ventilation grill on the top of the oven.

請勿覆蓋機身上方的通風架。

| 為什麼還能這樣翻 2 ···

　　英文句子中，若突然字母以大寫的方式表達時，表示強調語氣。在中文譯文中，亦可以放大字體、套以不同顏色，或加上底線來表示強調語氣。若譯作「機身上方的通風架請勿覆蓋」雖不算錯誤，但因本文為使用說明，將「請」，和「請勿」置於句首是更為恰當的譯法。

微波爐正確操作說明

一・使用本設備前，先詳細閱讀操作說明。

二・移除所有外包裝。

三・置於寬敞平坦表面，且四面通風。

四・使用前先移除所有內包裝。

五・將插頭插入 110 伏特的壁裝電源插座。

六・**請勿**覆蓋機身上方的通風架。

七・**請勿**在微波爐運轉中開啟門把。

6-3 「廣告傳單」要怎麼翻？

關鍵技巧　「吸引消費者」是關鍵！ ▶

關鍵例句搶先看 ▶

Come and enjoy a relaxing weekend at our newly opened spa resort in Changhua.

歡迎蒞臨我們位於彰化的新開幕渡假村，享受放鬆的週末吧！

基礎技巧提點

1 廣告性質的內容，需適時加以恰當並符合吸引客戶的用詞。

2 英文折扣數的寫法為扣除百分之幾的方式表示，中文則是以乘於百分之幾的方式表示，容易發生誤譯的問題。如：「20% off」，表示「八折」。

3 各國貨幣符號盡量譯出譯名，若是常用且辨識率高的貨幣，可只以符號譯出。台灣貨幣「新台幣」的符號「NT.」，在國際間並不屬於辨識率高的符號，但可考量譯文若以台灣讀者為主，則僅以符號表示。

試著翻翻看▶ 試著翻畫底線的部分

❶ Come and enjoy a relaxing weekend at our newly opened spa resort in Changhua. The only 5 star spa resort in Changhua with its own private beach. Put your feet up, unwind and enjoy our superior service with our never to be repeated offer of two nights for the price of one during the entire month of April. ❷ Special family weekend packages are also available throughout the summer with prices as low as NT$15,000 for two nights. That's over 30% off our regular price.

Check out our website at www.5starsparesort.com.tw for full prices and availability.

❶ _____

_____

_____

❷ _____

_____

❶ Come and enjoy a relaxing weekend at our newly opened spa resort in Changhua.

歡迎蒞臨我們位於彰化的新開幕渡假村，享受放鬆的週末吧！

| 為什麼這樣翻 1 ·······································

　　廣告性質的內容，需適時加以恰當並符合吸引客戶的用詞。依文章內容可以知道，這是屬於飯店服務業的廣告，**因此需在譯文加入服務業慣用的招呼語－「歡迎蒞臨」，將使得譯文符合飯店服務業的領域。**將廣告文首句句尾改為驚嘆號，帶入吶喊、疾呼的情緒，使內容更加有張力。

❷ Special family weekend packages are also available throughout the summer with prices as low as NT$15,000 for two nights. That's over 30% off our regular price.

夏季的親子週末套裝行程，住宿兩晚，房價只要新台幣一萬五千元。低於一般訂房的七折價格。

| 為什麼這樣翻 2 ┈┈┈┈┈┈┈┈┈┈┈┈┈┈┈┈┈┈┈┈┈┈┈

　　各國貨幣符號盡量譯出譯名。台灣貨幣「新台幣」的符號「NT.」，在國際間並不屬於辨識率高的符號，故應譯出譯名「新台幣」，以免造成讀者的誤解。「30% off」即中文的「七折」。「for two nights」的譯文，需符合飯店服務業的用語，譯作「住宿兩晚」，不可直譯為「兩個晚上」。

❶ Come and enjoy a relaxing weekend at our newly opened spa resort in Changhua.

歡迎蒞臨我們位於彰化的新開幕渡假村，享受愜意的週末。

| 為什麼還能這樣翻 1 ⋯⋯⋯⋯⋯⋯⋯⋯⋯⋯⋯⋯⋯⋯⋯⋯⋯⋯⋯⋯⋯⋯

　　「enjoy a relaxing weekend」，亦可譯作「享受愜意的週末」，句尾若以句號表示，就不需加上語助詞「吧」。此譯法會顯得較死板，較無法表達活潑熱情敬邀的語氣，但譯文仍為正確譯文。廣告用語，只要夠簡潔並具吸引力，皆屬好的譯法，有時還可以當地或各國文化時下的流行用字做為譯文的選擇。

❷ Special family weekend packages are also available throughout the summer with prices as low as NT$15,000 for two nights. That's over 30% off our regular price.

親子週末套裝行程，夏季優惠住宿兩晚，房價只要新台幣一萬五千元；省下 30%以上的住宿費用。

為什麼還能這樣翻 2

「... for two nights. That's over 30% off...」，亦可譯作「……房價只要新台幣一萬五千元；省下 30％以上的住宿費用。」，以分號連接獨立句子，比起句號，更能顯示出兩個句子之間的相關性。「夏季的親子週末套裝行程，住宿兩晚」，亦可譯作「親子週末套裝行程，夏季優惠住宿兩晚」。

全文翻譯

歡迎蒞臨我們位於彰化的新開幕渡假村，享受放鬆的週末吧！擁有私人沙灘，全彰化唯一的五星級渡假村。躺在椅背上，放鬆心情，盡情享受我們提供的精緻服務。四月份入住，還可享住宿兩晚，第二晚免費的優惠，僅此一檔。夏季的親子週末套裝行程，住宿兩晚，房價只要新台幣一萬五千元。低於一般訂房的七折價格。

詳細房價請參閱渡假村網站 www.5starsparesort.com.tw

「對話」怎麼翻？

關鍵技巧　模擬「對話」的口氣！ ▶

關鍵例句搶先看 ◉

No, I'm just saying just because you're on foot doesn't mean you can wander about wherever you like concentrating on your cellphone.

我不是這個意思，我只是說，你不能因為自己是徒步，所以就只顧著看手機，隨意漫步。

基礎技巧提點

1 本文為兩人之間的皆以第二人稱稱呼對方的對話，為爭論、互相指責的語氣。

2 省略號（又稱刪節號）「……」，也用於表示語氣停頓的狀態。

3 驚嘆號「！」，用於表達抗議的情緒。

4 **譯意不譯字，更不應逐字譯，需依文章內容與背景，譯文應以最貼近情境的詮釋方式呈現。**

✏️ 試著翻翻看▶ 試著翻畫底線的部分

A: Hey! Watch out. You nearly knocked me over!

B: I'm sorry. I didn't see you in time.

A: You should be paying more attention to where you are going. You're going to hurt somebody.

B: Well...Maybe you shouldn't be walking in the cycle lane.

A: Oh...So it's my fault now, is it?

B: ❶ No, I'm just saying just because you're on foot doesn't mean you can wander about wherever you like concentrating on your cellphone.

A: ❷ You're one to talk I can hear your headphones from here. Maybe you should turn them down and pay more attention to where you're going, too!

❶ _____

_____

_____

❷ _____

_____

❶ No, I'm just saying just because you're on foot doesn't mean you can wander about wherever you like concentrating on your cellphone.

我不是這個意思，我只是說，你不能因為自己是徒步，所以就只顧著看手機，隨意漫步。

| 為什麼這樣翻 1 ....

「No,」的譯文若只直譯作「不；不是」，就會馬上提升語氣中的爭論情緒，與接續的「I'm just saying」，其語意表示所表達的某件事，並非嚴厲的指責或指控，而是輕鬆、閒聊的語氣有衝突，故譯作「我不是這個意思」、「我只是說」。「wander about」是漫步的意思。

❷ You're one to talk I can hear your headphones from here.

你還好意思說！我從這裡就能聽到從你耳機傳出來的聲音。

| 為什麼這樣翻 2 ……………………

　　從文章內容可判斷出第一位主角因差點被撞倒，因而從一開始的口氣便不是很好，因此可在他的敘述中，加入驚嘆號，表示抗議的情緒。「You're one to talk」，譯作具責備口吻的「你還好意思說！」

　　「hear your headphones」，雖然字面上僅為「聽到你的耳機」，當我們這麼表達時，當然是指「耳機裡傳出來的聲音」，因為原文並未敘述第二位主角是在聽音樂或是廣播，所以僅加入譯出文「聲音」，才不會影響譯文的正確性。

❶ No, I'm just saying just because you're on foot doesn't mean you can wander about wherever you like concentrating on your cellphone.

我沒這個意思，我是說，你不能因為自己徒步，還顧著看手機，就隨意走上自行車道。

| 為什麼還能這樣翻 1 ⋯⋯⋯⋯⋯⋯⋯⋯⋯⋯⋯⋯⋯⋯⋯⋯⋯⋯⋯⋯⋯⋯

　　譯文的語氣維持非嚴厲指責或指控，而是以輕鬆、閒聊，甚至有些規勸的語氣來表示。**「我不是這個意思，我只是說⋯⋯」，亦可譯作「我沒這個意思，我是說⋯⋯」，或是「我不是這個意思，只是⋯⋯」。**

❷ You're one to talk I can hear your headphones from here.

你還敢說呢！我從這裡就聽得到你耳機的聲音。

| 為什麼還能這樣翻 2 ⋯⋯⋯⋯⋯⋯⋯⋯⋯⋯⋯⋯⋯⋯⋯⋯⋯⋯⋯⋯⋯⋯

　　「我從這裡就能聽到從你耳機傳出來的聲音」，亦可譯作「我從這裡就聽得到你耳機的聲音」，不會有令人產生誤解之虞。「你還好意思說！」，亦可譯作「你還敢説

呢！」，或是「你還敢講！」。

A：喂！小心一點。你差點撞倒我了！

B：對不起。我沒有及時看到你。

A：你應該多留心自己的行進路線。你這樣可是會傷到人吶！

B：哦…或許你不應該走在自行車道上。

A：噢，所以現在是我的錯囉？

B：我不是這個意思，我只是説，你不能因為自己是徒步，所以就只顧著看手機，隨意漫步。

A：你還好意思説！我從這裡就能聽到從你耳機傳出來的聲音。也許你該把音量調低，多留心自己的行進路線才是！

「清單」怎麼翻？

「簡單」、「清楚」是關鍵！ ▶

關鍵例句搶先看 ◉

We are charging the following items for your stay with us:

我們將依您於住宿期間的消費項目收費：

基礎技巧提點

1 電子郵件、商業往來信件內容所提及的人名、組織名稱，不需音譯為中文譯名，僅以原文表示即可。

2 「VAT」是「value added tax」的縮寫，是「增值稅」的意思。

3 內容為帳單性質的文件，其數值與百分比符號，皆以阿拉伯數字與百分比符號表示，不以中文字形式譯出。

4 視內文涉及的行業類別，在不更改原意的情況下，譯文需用以慣用行話與用詞。服務業慣於以「貴賓」、「您」稱呼顧客。

✏ 試著翻翻看▶ 試著翻畫底線的部分

Booking Ref: A72832

Invoice Number: 00005

Invoice date: 8/19/2016

Dear Mr. Adams

❶ We are charging the following items for your stay with us:

8/16/2016 – 8/19/2016

Superior double room$170 per night	$510
Dinner 8/16	$49
Room service 8/17	$31
Wellness special	
Massage 8/16	$50
Mud bath 8/17	$50
Sub total	$690
VAT 7%	$48
Total	$638

We have received a cash payment for the invoice amount.

❷ Thank you for staying at Raythorn Hotels and Resorts.

We look forward to seeing you again.

❶ _____

❷ _____

❶ We are charging the following items for your stay with us:

我們將依您於住宿期間的消費項目收費：

| 為什麼這樣翻 1 ···

冒號「：」用於引語、解釋、系列之前。

依原文內容，可以得知這是由飯店渡假村發給住宿房客的信件，在飯店「stay」即為「住宿」，因此可直接將「the following items」譯作「住宿期間的消費項目」。「with us」的省略不譯，因為已在句首提過「我們」（指飯店方面），且譯文需符合飯店服務業慣用語，因此不用再譯作「……在我們這裡……」。

❷ Thank you for staying at Raythorn Hotels and Resorts. We look forward to seeing you again.

感謝您選擇 Raythorn 飯店渡假村，我們期待您的再次來訪。

| 為什麼這樣翻 2

「Thank you for staying at Raythorn Hotels and Resorts」，以及「We look forward to seeing you again」，是每飯店和服務業常用的用語，若直譯作「感謝您住宿在 Raythorn 飯店渡假村」跟「我們期待再次看到你」，並不符合飯店服務業的慣用語，需以站在該服務業的角度，以最合宜也最貼切的方式，加以修飾譯文。

❶ We are charging the following items for your stay with us:

以下是您於住宿期間的消費明細：

| 為什麼還能這樣翻 1 ·······································

　　原譯文「我們將依您於住宿期間的消費項目收費：」，亦可譯作「以下是您於住宿期間的消費明細：」。只要是「消費」，就會有使用者付費的認知，因此省略「We are charging...」這部分的譯文，不影響原意。

❷ Thank you for staying at Raythorn Hotels and Resorts. We look forward to seeing you again.

感謝您選擇 Raythorn 飯店渡假村，我們期待與您再次相會。

| 為什麼還能這樣翻 2 ·······································

　　「We look forward to seeing you again」，原譯文以「我們期待您的再次來訪」表示，較符合一般時下的口頭說話方式。譯作「我們期待與您再次相會」，則是有些略顯拗口。

訂房單號：A72832

發票編號：00005

發票日期：2016 年 8 月 19 日

親愛的 Adams 先生您好，

我們將依您於住宿期間的消費項目收費：

住宿期間 2016 年 8 月 16 日至 2016 年 8 月 19 日

精緻雙人房（兩大床） 房價 170 美金／每晚	510 美金
8 月 16 日晚餐	49 美金
8 月 17 日客房服務	31 美金
健康養身項目	
8 月 16 日按摩	50 美金
8 月 17 日泥浴	50 美金
小計	690 美金
另計 7%增值稅	48 美金
總計	638 美金

我們已收到您以現金支付上述款項。

感謝您選擇 Raythorn 飯店渡假村，我們期待您的再次來訪。

關鍵技巧

「用字正式」是關鍵！ ▶

關鍵例句搶先看 ▶

It was a pleasure to meet you and to discuss your qualifications.

很榮幸認識你，並討論你所具備的條件。

基礎技巧提點

1 一般商業性質的書信往來，若以第二人稱稱呼對方時，通常將對方稱作「你」。若是想突顯客氣或是尊敬，則會寫作「您」。

2 「should」在本文等同「in case」，意即「以防萬一」。

3 書信文件內容的專有名詞，若無固有譯名，則以原文譯出即可。

4 中文書信在最後的屬名部分，習慣將頭銜、職稱放在屬名之前。

✏️ 試著翻翻看▶ **試著翻畫底線的部分**

Dear Mr. Collins

Thank you for your application for employment at Reed Accountants as an accounting clerk.

❶ It was a pleasure to meet you and to discuss your qualifications. We have reviewed your background and experience and unfortunately we are unable to offer you the position because another candidate more closely matched our needs. ❷ We will keep your CV on file should another position become available.

We appreciate your interest in Reed Accounting and wish you success in your job search.

Sincerely,

Jocey Hargreaves

Human Resources Manager

❶ _____

❷ _____

❶ It was a pleasure to meet you and to discuss your qualifications.

很榮幸認識你，並討論你所具備的條件。

| 為什麼這樣翻 1 ⋯⋯⋯⋯⋯⋯⋯⋯⋯⋯⋯⋯⋯⋯⋯⋯⋯⋯⋯⋯⋯⋯

「It was a pleasure to...」，其「It」是代名詞主詞，表示「to meet you and to discuss your qualifications」這件事，「was a pleasure」。譯文不可逐字直譯作「它是榮幸的認識你，……」。「qualification」有「資格」、「條件」、「能力」的意思，其譯文需視內容，選擇最恰當的用詞。

❷ We will keep your CV on file should another position become available.

我們會將你的履歷存檔，以備日後尚有會計員職缺。

| **為什麼這樣翻 2** ....

　　應視實際內容，適時加入譯出文，使句子更完整且通順。「should another position become available」，其「should」是「以防萬一；以備不時之需」的意思。在譯文加入「日後」兩字，符合本句英文以未來式敘述尚未發生的事情，也呼應了「以備不時之需」的語意。

　　「another position」，其「another」是代名詞，表示第一段的「accounting clerk」。

❶ It was a pleasure to meet you and to discuss your qualifications.

很榮幸跟你會談，討論你所具備的能力。

| 為什麼還能這樣翻 1 ⋯⋯⋯⋯⋯⋯⋯⋯⋯⋯⋯⋯⋯⋯⋯⋯⋯⋯⋯⋯⋯⋯

「a pleasure to meet you」，亦可譯作「很榮幸跟你會談」。「your qualifications」，亦可譯作「你所具備的能力」，或是「你所具備的資格條件」。

❷ We will keep your CV on file should another position become available.

我們將存檔保留你的履歷，以備將來出現另一職缺。

| 為什麼還能這樣翻 2 ⋯⋯⋯⋯⋯⋯⋯⋯⋯⋯⋯⋯⋯⋯⋯⋯⋯⋯⋯⋯⋯⋯

「keep your CV on file」，亦可譯作「存檔保留」，但在文字敘述上，仍顯得有些多餘，因「存檔」即有「保留」之意。「以備日後尚有會計員職缺」，亦可作「以備將來出現另一職缺」。

親愛的 Collins 先生你好,

謝謝你向 Reed 會計事務所提出會計員一職的申請。

很榮幸認識你,並討論你所具備的條件。我們已複審你的背景與經歷,不過很抱歉,我們無法提供你這個職缺,因為另一位申請人更符合我們的需求。我們會將你的履歷存檔,以備日後尚有會計員職缺。

我們十分感激你對 Reed 會計事務所的青睞,並祝你找工作順利。

誠摯地

Jocey Hargreaves 人力資源部經理敬啟

6-7 「笑話」怎麼翻？

「搞懂英文笑點」是關鍵！ ▶

關鍵例句搶先看 ●

A teacher wanted to teach her students about self-esteem, so she asked anyone who thought they were stupid to stand up.

老師想教學生有關自尊的課題，於是便要求認為自己笨的學生站起來。

基礎技巧提點

1 在不更改原意的情況下，譯文可適時以標點符號突顯語氣情緒，或語助詞，增加笑話的精采程度。

2 笑話常以諧音、拆解字義的方式，達到娛人的效果。不同語言之間的各國笑話，常在譯作另一種語言時，因而失去其精采程度。因此，翻譯笑話時，需抓到要點，並保持譯文的精確簡短，唯常需附註解釋，以助讀者意會並了解。

1 ❶ <u>A teacher wanted to teach her students about self-esteem, so she asked anyone who thought they were stupid to stand up. One kid stood up and the teacher was surprised, so she asked him, "Why did you stand up?" He answered, "I didn't want to leave you standing up by yourself."</u>

2 If you ever get onto a plane and recognize a friend called Jack, don't shout 'Hi, Jack!'

3 A: Why can't you trust an atom?

　B: Because they make up literally everything.

4 A: How do fish get high?

　B: Seaweed.

5 ❷ <u>A man got hit in the head with a can of Coke. Thank goodness it was a soft drink.</u>

❶ _____

❷ _____

❶ A teacher wanted to teach her students about self-esteem, so she asked anyone who thought they were stupid to stand up.

老師想教學生有關自尊的課題，於是便要求認為自己笨的學生站起來。

| 為什麼這樣翻 1 ....

「A teacher wanted to teach her students about self-esteem」，若直譯為「老師想教學生有關自尊」，**會使得句子像是還沒結束般地懸著，因內容背景是在學校的教學，因此在譯文加入「課題」，讓譯文更具完整性。**「ask」在這為「要求」的意思。

❷ A man got hit in the head with a can of Coke.

Thank goodness it was a soft drink.

男人被罐裝可樂砸到頭。

謝天謝地，幸好它是軟的飲料。

註：（「soft drink」即無酒精飲料。將固有名詞拆解，字義即變成軟的「soft」和飲料「drink」）。

| 為什麼這樣翻 2 ⋯⋯⋯⋯⋯⋯⋯⋯⋯⋯⋯⋯⋯⋯⋯⋯⋯⋯⋯⋯⋯⋯⋯

　　當笑話是將某特定涵意的語詞，以拆解文字意思，或是取諧音的方式達到娛人效果時，需以圓括弧加註解釋，以助讀者更深入了解好笑的部分在哪；**若只採直譯字面上的意思，很難讓人意會。笑話與俚語、成語、慣用語一樣，皆需了解其典故與蘊涵的寓意與智慧，方能體會箇中意涵，達到讓人會心一笑的境界。**

❶ A teacher wanted to teach her students about self-esteem, so she asked anyone who thought they were stupid to stand up.

老師想教學生自尊是什麼，於是便要求自認不聰明的學生起立。

| 為什麼還能這樣翻 1 ⋯⋯⋯⋯⋯⋯⋯⋯⋯⋯⋯⋯⋯⋯⋯⋯⋯⋯⋯⋯⋯

「老師想教學生有關自尊的課題」，亦可譯作「老師想教學生自尊是什麼」。「認為自己笨」，亦可譯作「自認不聰明」、「認為自己是笨蛋」、「自認頭腦不好」。「站起來」，亦可譯作「起立」。

❷ A man got hit in the head with a can of Coke.

Thank goodness it was a soft drink.

男人被一罐可樂砸到頭。

感謝老天，它是軟的飲料。

註：（「soft drink」即無酒精飲料。將固有名詞拆解，字義即變成軟的「soft」和飲料「drink」）。

| 為什麼還能這樣翻 2

「男人被罐裝可樂砸到頭」，亦可譯作「男人被一罐可樂砸到頭」。「謝天謝地，幸好它是軟的飲料」，亦可譯作「感謝老天，它是軟的飲料」、「還好它是軟的飲料」。

全文翻譯

1 老師想教學生有關「自尊」的課題，於是便要求認為自己笨的學生站起來。一位學生馬上起立，老師一臉訝異地詢問他：「你為什麼要站起來呢？」他回答道：「因為我不想留你獨自一個人站著。」

2 要是你在搭飛機時，遇到名字叫 Jack 的朋友，千萬別大喊：「嗨！Jack。」

註：（音同「hijack」，「劫機」的意思）。

3 A：為什麼不能信任分子？

B：因為整個世界都是他們編造出來的。

4 A：魚要怎麼讓自己飄飄欲仙？

B：抽海裡的大麻。

註：（「seaweed」是名詞，海藻。取其諧音與拆解字義，即變成海「sea」和大麻「weed」）。

5 男人被罐裝可樂砸到頭。

謝天謝地，幸好它是軟的飲料。

註：（「soft drink」即無酒精飲料。將固有名詞拆解，字義即變成軟的「soft」和飲料「drink」）。

Learn Smart! 066

中英互譯筆譯技巧：基礎

作　　者	連緯晏 Wendy Lien、Matthew Gunton
發 行 人	周瑞德
執行總監	齊心瑀
企劃編輯	饒美君
校　　對	編輯部
封面構成	高鍾琪

內頁構成	菩薩蠻數位文化有限公司
印　　製	大亞彩色印刷製版股份有限公司
初　　版	2016 年 10 月
定　　價	新台幣 369 元
出　　版	倍斯特出版事業有限公司
電　　話	(02) 2351-2007
傳　　真	(02) 2351-0887
地　　址	100 台北市中正區福州街 1 號 10 樓之 2
E - m a i l	best.books.service@gmail.com
網　　址	www.bestbookstw.com

港澳地區總經銷	泛華發行代理有限公司
地　　　　址	香港新界將軍澳工業邨駿昌街 7 號 2 樓
電　　　　話	(852) 2798-2323
傳　　　　真	(852) 2796-5471

國家圖書館出版品預行編目資料

中英互譯筆譯技巧. 基礎 / 連緯晏,
Matthew Gunton 著. -- 初版. -- 臺北市 :
倍斯特, 2016.10
　面 ; 　公分. -- (Learn smart ; 66)
ISBN 978-986-92855-9-9(平裝)

1. 英語 2. 翻譯

805.1　　　　　　　105017439